PRAISE FOR MELANIE CHENG

Room for a Stranger

'Beautifully done. Melanie Cheng's
wisdom is just delightful…She cannot
change the world but the warmth of her affection
for lonely people will help to do just that.'
SYDNEY MORNING HERALD

'An impressive and delicately crafted novel
from one of Australia's most talented new voices.'
BOOKS+PUBLISHING

'With such rich characterisation and beautiful prose,
this is a wonderful, contemporary Australian novel.'
READINGS MONTHLY

'*Room for a Stranger*'s beauty lies in confronting
the unknown parts of ourselves…a timely reminder
of all the badness in the world, and a reminder that
we don't need to give into it if we don't want to.'
KILL YOUR DARLINGS

'A beautifully written novel about how the stories we tell
ourselves can get us stuck and how opening our lives to others
might jolt us free again. Melanie Cheng offers both razor-sharp
insight into the flaws and foibles of ordinary people and a deep
warmth and tenderness for them. *Room for a Stranger* is that
rare thing: a novel which stings and soothes all at once.'
EMILY MAGUIRE

'This is an impressive and quietly significant book.'
MONTHLY

Australia Day

ROOM FOR A STRANGER

Melanie Cheng is a writer and general practitioner. She was born in Adelaide, grew up in Hong Kong and now lives in Melbourne. Her debut collection of short stories, *Australia Day*, won the Victorian Premier's Literary Award for an Unpublished Manuscript in 2016 and the Victorian Premier's Literary Award for Fiction in 2018. *Room for a Stranger* is her first novel.

ROOM FOR A STRANGER

MELANIE CHENG

TEXT PUBLISHING MELBOURNE AUSTRALIA

textpublishing.com.au

The Text Publishing Company
Swann House
22 William Street
Melbourne Victoria 3000
Australia

Published by The Text Publishing Company, 2019
Reprinted 2019

Cover design by W. H. Chong
Cover illustration by iStock
Page design by Jessica Horrocks
Typeset by J&M Typesetting

Printed and bound in Australia by Griffin Press, part of Ovato, an accredited ISO/NZS 14001:2004 Environmental Management System printer

ISBN: 9781925773545 (paperback)
ISBN: 9781925774351 (ebook)

A catalogue record for this book is available from the National Library of Australia

This book is printed on paper certified against the Forest Stewardship Council® Standards. Griffin Press holds FSC chain-of-custody certification SGS-COC-005088. FSC promotes environmentally responsible, socially beneficial and economically viable management of the world's forests.

For Rani, Alyssa and Toby

SEPTEMBER

1

She couldn't forget his eyes. Cold blue with a hint of crazy, or drugs—probably that nasty stuff they called ice, which made people pick their skin. God knows what he saw when he looked back at her that night. Something other than an old woman in a dressing-gown and sheepskin slippers. Why else would he have fled? When the police finally apprehended him, they found a switchblade in his sneakers. Meg wasn't sure why the officer—a small woman with a severe bun—had told her that. The whole confrontation must have lasted less than a minute, and yet here she was, months later, with the boy's pockmarked face still etched behind her lids.

The comfort she had once gleaned from the faded sticker in the window—*Warning! This house is protected by a 24-hour monitored alarm system*—now seemed delusional. At night every black pane of glass concealed a lurking predator. Every growl of a car engine announced a fresh criminal. A few times a month Meg had to take a sleeping tablet just to get a few hours' rest.

Judith, her next-door neighbour, had suggested she get a dog, but a dog would need walking and there was the issue of her knees. Not to mention that Meg hated dogs—she couldn't bear their wet noses and long, undulating tongues. Meg was a bird person. Atticus, her African grey parrot, was smarter than most people she knew but, alas, no use against knife-wielding burglars.

Meg pulled herself up from her recliner. She'd been sitting there, with the lights off, since six o'clock. She opened the curtains, flooding the lounge room with sun. Dust motes whirled like tiny galaxies before her eyes. If she had time later, maybe she would wipe down the mantelpiece, but right now she needed a cup of tea. She walked to the kitchen, flicked the switch on the kettle. There was a rustle from Atticus's cage, which sat on a table behind the door to the kitchen. Meg removed the cover. The parrot drew his head out of the toilet roll she'd given him yesterday to play with. Startled, he stared at her with his pale yellow eyes. 'Top of the morning to you!' he squawked. Meg laughed. She stuck her finger through the bars of the cage and scratched the scalloped grey feathers around his neck.

On the fridge door, beside a letter from Rakesh—the boy she sponsored in Bangladesh—was a photo of an older boy, a young man really, Chinese, with a stern, unsmiling face. She freed the photo from the magnet as she retrieved the milk from the fridge. The milk was long-life, which she hated, but she couldn't get to the shops often enough to buy fresh milk. Perhaps the Chinese boy could help with that.

Meg groaned as she sat down at the kitchen table. While she sipped her tea she studied the photo. He was twenty-one, she knew that much, though he looked much younger. If she'd been asked to describe him, she would say his eyes were dark brown, almost black—but it was hard to tell through his glasses. She could just make out a couple of acne scars marring his chin. He wasn't handsome, but he was pleasant-looking. Meg covered his serious lips with her hand, imagined a smile.

The clock on the wall read ten. Andy wasn't due to arrive until twelve-thirty. She would need that much time to shower and dress and make herself presentable. Soon enough—if they both agreed to sign up to the homeshare arrangement—he would see her on the couch in her pyjamas, but Meg had always maintained that first impressions were important. She finished her tea, washed and dried her cup. Perhaps he could do the dishes, she thought, when he had settled in. Ten hours of help a week was the agency agreement. She wouldn't ask him to help with the washing—she didn't fancy a stranger handling her undies—and she couldn't assume a man knew his way around the kitchen, so cooking was a question mark. She felt overcome by the decisions suddenly confronting her. There were so many details to be considered.

She made her way down the dimly lit corridor to her bedroom. On her way she looked into the room she'd set up for her visitor. It had been her sister's bedroom, and even now, emptied of its adjustable hospital bed and various paraphernalia—the Western Bulldogs scarves, the bowls of potpourri, the dreamy Marc Chagall prints—it was still her sister's. There were clues, like the lines marking Helen's height on the back of the bedroom door, and the yellow tape on the wall where there had once been a Rolling Stones poster. It had been Meg's room too, a long time ago. Before her sister was born. Before the accident.

Meg took off her dressing-gown and flannelette pyjamas. Thanks to Helen, the bathroom had been fitted with rails long before Meg had needed them. They came in handy now, with the arthritis in her knees. Meg sat down on the shower stool and turned on the tap. She closed her eyes and felt the needles of hot water across her back. These days she limited her showers to three a week. Water was expensive, and besides, a daily wash was excessive. It'd been years since she'd done anything strenuous enough to work up a sweat—except gardening, and even then, until recently a handyman had done the heavy pruning every couple of months.

As Meg sat on her stool—the water flattening what little hair still clung to her head—she stared through the window at the branches of the jacaranda. They were bare now, but every November for as long as she could remember, the tree had been marking the years with a canopy of purple petals. She recalled sitting with her mother beneath the violet flowers the morning her sister had been discharged from hospital. Meg was sixteen at the time, but she'd rested her head in her mother's lap like a baby.

As she dried herself with the towel, she took stock of the

bathroom. She'd never been fussy about her appearance—she'd only painted her nails once, at Helen's insistence, before a friend's wedding—and yet somehow the bath and the sink were still lined with pastel-coloured bottles. Shampoo, conditioner, perfume, a tube of expired pawpaw cream her doctor had recommended for a rash. She worried that all the citrus and floral aromas would overwhelm the boy. The last man to have lived here was Meg's father, thirty years ago. Aside from a couple of photos and his golf clubs—buried behind rolls of wrapping paper in the linen cupboard—there was not a trace of him left inside the house.

Meg sprayed some perfume on her wrists and walked, naked, to her bedroom. Ordinarily she would cover herself with a towel but—knowing nudity would soon be out of the question—today she took one last liberty. In the bedroom she put on her bra, fastening the clasp at the front before rotating it around to the back. It'd been years since she'd had anyone around to help her dress. For the most part she managed. Only once had she had to cut herself out of a skirt when a bit of fabric got caught in the zip.

She stood back and appraised her wardrobe. It was a drab collection of blouses and skirts and high-waisted pants. Helen had been the loud dresser in their little family. Meg's sister loved nothing more than drawing attention to herself. Her wheelchair had been adorned with so many stickers and tassels, it had acquired the nickname Dame Edna Everage. Now, contemplating her boring clothes, Meg remembered how people used to mistake her for Helen's nurse. Unwittingly, she had adopted the uniform—dark, inoffensive colours with prim collars and soft pleats. Clothes that helped her disappear into the background, like a stagehand, or a puppeteer. Only it had always been Helen tugging away at the strings.

Amid all the black Meg saw a flash of red. She pulled out a scarlet blouse she'd worn years ago to a New Year's Eve party. She slipped it on and considered herself in the mirror. The bright colour brought some much-needed life to her cheeks. She coupled it with a dark skirt to disguise her belly—a bulge she recognised on every woman over fifty, and just one of many clues to her advancing age. There were also her jowly cheeks, the crepe-paper skin on her hands and the spider veins around her ankles. It would be good to share her house with someone young—someone who didn't groan as they got out of bed in the morning, who didn't fall asleep at eight pm with their mouth open in front of the television. As hard as it was going to be, Meg felt certain she'd made the right decision.

2

An Uber driver picked Andy up from Spencer Street. He was moving out of his studio apartment, the only home he'd known in Melbourne. His aunt had driven all the way from Geelong the night before to pick up what little furniture he owned—a small couch, a futon and an LCD TV—and pack it into her trailer. All that remained was a duffel bag full of clothes and two large cardboard boxes. Andy loaded the boxes into the boot.

As they drove, Andy leant back and surveyed the view through his window. Office blocks and 7-Elevens gave way to weatherboard houses. The suburbs still surprised him—the cartoonish bungalows, the easily scaled waist-high timber fences. He'd grown up in an apartment with bars on every window—a barrier to keep the children in and the burglars out. There'd also been a security guard manning the lobby day and night. Never mind that the guard was elderly, unarmed and partly deaf—in the event of an emergency, he could alert the closest police station with the push of a button. This helped the residents all sleep a little more soundly.

It was Andy's aunt who'd suggested the homeshare program. Andy wasn't keen on the idea, but he wasn't entirely opposed to it, either. His father had been forced to sell his cleaning business in Hong Kong, and his parents' savings were barely enough to pay for the remaining two years of his course. If Andy wanted to complete his studies there was no other option. Besides, he knew what it was like to live with an old person—when he was ten he'd had to share a room with his grandfather. He remembered the way his yeh yeh had snored, saliva hanging in shiny tendrils from his mouth, but he also recalled how his grandfather had helped him with his model aeroplanes—the calm and patient way he'd overcome his tremor to paint a miniature B-25 propeller.

The Uber driver pulled over in the middle of a quiet street. Andy could hardly see the house, which was shrouded in trees and bushes. He could just make out a stone birdbath through the heavy curtain of leaves.

'This is the place,' the driver said.

Andy got out and retrieved his cardboard boxes from the boot. He stacked the boxes on the footpath before unlatching the wrought-iron gate, which announced his arrival with a squeak. The mailbox was choked with old catalogues, hanging wet and limp from its metal mouth. For a moment he considered bringing them in. Was that the type of thing he'd be expected to do now? Ten hours of work a week suddenly seemed like a lot. Andy hitched the duffel bag onto his shoulder and picked up the boxes. He followed the concrete path to the peeling front door. On hearing the Uber speed away, he felt a profound sense of regret. He was only ten kilometres from the city, but it may as well have been a hundred. When he inhaled, his nostrils filled with the smell of damp leaves, burnt toast and decomposing vegetables. He considered calling another Uber to take him back to the city, but then he remembered he only had fifty dollars until his mother transferred more money on Thursday.

His finger shook as he pressed the doorbell, which, instead of ringing, played an instrumental version of 'Auld Lang Syne'. He heard the shriek of a bird, followed by the shuffle of slippered feet. Andy took a deep breath. On the other side of the door lay his new home and the stranger he'd be sharing it with. Feeling exposed, he picked up one of the boxes and held it before him like a shield.

3

The boy who greeted her on the doorstep was holding a large cardboard box. There was a duffel bag slung across his shoulder and another cardboard box at his feet. The homeshare coordinator had told Meg that today was just an introduction—a chance to get to know each other before making a final decision—and yet the young man standing before her looked ready to move in.

'You must be Andy,' she said. Even in slippers, Meg was a few inches taller than him.

He stared at her across the lid of the box, nodded. There were Chinese characters scrawled on one side of the carton. Meg wondered if the boy spoke any English.

'I'm Margaret Hughes, but you can call me Meg.'

Andy nodded again.

Helpless, Meg ushered him inside. While she held the door open she watched him set the box down on the floor and take off his sneakers. He entered wearing only his socks. As she led him down the hall, she saw the house through fresh eyes. For the first time she noticed the cracks in the plaster around the doors and the balding carpet in front of the hatstand. She swiped at a cobweb clinging to a photo frame in the hallway and led him to Helen's old bedroom.

'This will be your room,' Meg said, pausing at the door, 'if everything works out.' If he was taken aback by her hesitancy, Andy didn't show it. He dumped the first box on the floor and hurried back down the hallway to fetch the other one. Meg retreated to the kitchen. She filled the kettle with water. Helen had always said there was nothing a cup of tea couldn't fix.

'Would you like a hot drink?' she called down the corridor, but there was no answer. When the kettle finished boiling, Meg tried again, a little louder: 'Do you drink tea?' But there was still no response. Only when she began walking towards the bedroom did he reply.

'No thank you.'

His voice surprised her—it was lower and more masculine than she'd expected.

Meg returned to the kitchen to prepare tea in her precise way, brewing the bag for two minutes before adding one level teaspoon of raw sugar. When she was done she sat at the kitchen table, holding the warm cup to her lips. Atticus, bored of the toilet roll, was attacking a shiny button with his beak.

Sensing Meg's eyes on him, he looked up and fluffed his ash-coloured feathers.

'Fine and dandy! Sugar candy!' he screeched.

Since Helen had died, three years ago, Atticus had been Meg's only companion. She'd shared a house with him for almost twenty-five years—longer than many marriages. But there had been a time when they were strangers. For a couple of years, Atticus had been the beloved pet of the Bishop family, who lived next door in a bright Californian bungalow. Meg and Helen would hear the parrot sometimes, in the backyard, singing with the children. When Mr Bishop's job had taken him overseas, the family had offered Atticus to Helen. Meg was hesitant at first—they'd just lost their mother to cancer, and everything was in a mess—but Helen had begged her, and Meg was no match for Helen's pleas. Besides, Meg believed the parrot was just the distraction they needed. Atticus fell head over heels in love with Helen, but he remained standoffish with Meg for months, biting her at every opportunity. Their relationship was more of a slow burn—a growing together, an affection born of necessity.

Now, as Atticus busied himself with a rolled-up ball of tinfoil, Meg listened to the noises coming from Helen's old room—the thud of textbooks, the creak of floorboards, the squeal of the mattress springs. It was a strange but comforting thing to hear another person moving about the house. Meg found her mobile phone on the counter and dialled the number for the homeshare coordinator. The woman, whose name was Pam, didn't pick up—it went straight through to her message bank.

'Hi, Pam. Margaret here, from number four Rose Street.' As she spoke she watched Atticus in his cage, scratching his back with his beak. 'I've met Andy and I think we'll get on well. I'll send you the paperwork tomorrow morning.'

Andy didn't come out of his room for two hours. In the meantime Meg finished her tea, read the newspaper and peeled the potatoes for dinner. Around three, she heard the flush of the toilet and the slap of Andy's feet across the floorboards. Before she knew it he was slouched in the doorway of the kitchen, looking at his plastic thongs.

'What kind of things do you like to eat?' Meg asked, turning from the sink to face him. She wiped her dirty hands with a tea towel.

'Anything, really. Rice. Noodles. Chips.' Andy flicked his eyes up towards her face before returning his gaze to the tiled floor.

Meg turned back to the potatoes soaking in the sink. 'I'm afraid I'm a meat-and-three-veg kind of girl.'

'I like meat,' Andy said, 'and vegetables.'

'Maybe one day you can cook me some noodles.' Meg went to the fridge and pulled out a tray of lamb chops. She glanced at Andy, who, at the mention of cooking, had stopped slouching and was now standing tall and stiff in the doorway. 'Or not. We don't have to decide straight away.' Meg couldn't remember the last time she'd eaten Chinese food. It was probably back when Helen was alive, before the engine in the old Holden had given up and they could still drive to the takeaway place up the road.

Andy sat down at the kitchen table. 'Your home is very big.'

Nobody had ever called Meg's home big before. It was a modest three-bedroom brick house with a small backyard and a leaky roof. They'd moved in soon after her dad had been promoted to manager at the textile company, a few months before Helen was born, seventy years ago. Over the years, nearby houses had been transformed into glassy spaces with exposed beams and Danish furniture, but Meg and Helen had made no improvements to theirs, other than the odd coat of paint every couple of decades. But Meg supposed it would be big compared with flats in Hong Kong. It made her wonder about the home the boy had left behind.

'I guess it's a good size,' she agreed. 'And your room? How do you like that?'

'It's fine,' Andy said, studying his fingernails.

Meg hated the word *fine*—Helen had only ever used it in the most sarcastic way. But it was possible Andy meant it sincerely. Meg's friend Jillian said that some cultures didn't indulge in sarcasm. Perhaps Chinese culture was one of them.

'Are you sure I can't get you a cup of tea or something?' she offered.

'Maybe just some water.'

Meg took a tumbler from the dish rack and filled it with water from the tap. As she put the glass down in front of Andy, a few drops splashed onto the table. Andy mopped them up with his sleeve.

'You'll dirty your clothes doing that,' Meg said. She pulled a tea towel from the handle of the oven and wiped away what

16

little water remained. 'How are you with cleaning?'

Andy sipped his water. 'My father used to own a cleaning business. He taught me how to polish mirrors.'

Meg thought of the mirrored cabinet above the sink in the bathroom and the full-length mirror in her bedroom. 'Well, that will take all of fifteen minutes a week. What else can you do?'

Andy frowned at the tiny bubbles on the surface of the water. It was hard to believe he was twenty-one. Meg sat down in the chair beside him.

'Do you like birds?' she asked and opened the door to Atticus's cage. The parrot climbed up her arm, coming to rest on her shoulder. 'Atticus,' Meg said, turning to rub her nose against his beak, 'this is Andy.'

Atticus tilted his head to the side and looked at the boy.

'In Hong Kong we have a bird market,' Andy said. 'People sell all kinds of birds there.'

'How rude!' Atticus shrieked, and made a tutting noise. The silver feathers around his neck pulsed.

Andy's eyes flashed wide. 'He talks?'

It had been a long time since Meg had introduced Atticus to anyone—she'd forgotten the thrill of it. 'Oh, yes. He's particularly fond of children's nursery rhymes.'

'Hey diddle diddle, the cat and the fiddle!' Atticus sang.

'That's amazing.'

'Humpty Dumpty sat on a wall! Humpty Dumpty had a great fall!' The bird made a whistling sound to indicate the egg plummeting towards the ground.

Andy smiled.

'You can pat him if you like,' Meg offered. She extended her arm and the bird sidestepped towards Andy. 'He loves a little scratch.'

Andy stuck out his index finger and poked the back of the parrot's head.

'Do you have any pets in Hong Kong?' Meg asked, just to keep the conversation going. It was clear from the tense way Andy was sitting that he'd never owned an animal.

'Hong Kong isn't like Australia. We don't have backyards.'

'Of course.'

'Mary, Mary, quite contrary, how does your garden grow?' Atticus interjected.

Andy pulled a tissue from his pocket and wiped his finger with it. 'What does his name mean?'

The bird stuck his head into the open end of Meg's sleeve. 'I'm not sure if it has a meaning,' she said. 'It's just a name. From the book *To Kill a Mockingbird*.'

'Atticus is a mockingbird?'

Meg laughed. 'No. He's an African grey parrot. But sometimes I do think he might be mocking me.' Andy seemed perplexed by this and Meg shook her head. 'It's a silly joke.'

Atticus emerged from Meg's sleeve, his feathers ruffled. 'Peekaboo! I see you!' he cried.

'He may not act like it, but he'll be turning thirty later this year,' Meg said.

'Thirty? That's older than me!'

'In captivity they can live up to fifty years—in the wild, up to eighty.'

'Wow.'

Satisfied that she had impressed her guest, Meg returned Atticus to his cage. She filled his bowl with seeds before turning back to the stove. 'I'd better get started on dinner,' she said.

That night Meg felt lighter than she had in years. Andy was quiet—painfully so—but the house felt different with him there. Atticus, too, seemed pleased with the new addition to the household. She couldn't remember the last time she'd seen him so excited. Meg had always suspected he'd become depressed—at the very least, severely bored—after Helen had passed away. He'd started plucking at the feathers on his belly, which she'd never seen him do while her sister was alive. No doubt the vet would approve of this new companion for Atticus too—someone younger and livelier than Meg. Not that Andy was particularly animated. In many ways he was like her—reserved and introverted—which was perfect, really, just what she'd been hoping for. Andy would save money on rent and Meg would sleep more soundly. It was a win-win situation.

4

Andy pulled the curtains closed and blew the dust from his fingers. Like so many in Hong Kong, he and his family had become fanatical about cleanliness and hygiene after the flu epidemics. They wore masks on public transport. They doused their hands with sanitiser after touching a door handle. When they were in a lift they used their elbows instead of their fingers to push the buttons.

All through dinner Andy had battled nausea at the memory of Mrs Hughes handling her pet parrot. He'd watched and waited for her to wash her hands, but she never had. When she finally put the plate of lamb chops in front of him, Andy felt ready to vomit. He'd chewed the meat for five minutes before spitting the remains into his napkin.

Now he pulled a packet of Wet Ones from his duffel bag and began wiping things down. He started with the window ledge, followed by the desk and the wooden headboard. When he was finished, he appraised the pile of blackened wipes in the rubbish bin with a revolted satisfaction. By ten o'clock, after he'd changed the sheets on the bed—replacing the rose-coloured quilt with his plain blue Ikea doona—some of his initial unease had abated. While he longed to have a shower and wash away all the grime, he worried the noise of the running water would wake the old lady.

As he lay in bed, Andy found himself wondering about his host. She was old—probably in her seventies—and most likely widowed. He assumed the room he was staying in had previously belonged to her daughter. It had marks recording a child's growth on the back of the door and the initials *H. H.* were scratched into a corner of the bedside table. He found it unnerving to be in such a feminine room. Andy was an only child. Apart from his mother—a serious woman who rarely wore make-up—he hadn't had much interaction with the opposite sex. At school he'd steered well clear of girls, the pretty ones in particular. He was suspicious of the way they could reduce his friends to a bunch of clowns with as little as a flick of their hair.

Andy patted the mattress. He felt the curve of springs, like a buried rib cage, beneath his fingertips. He supposed Mrs Hughes' daughter had brought boys into this bed. His best friend, Ming, had told him that Australian girls lost their virginity early. Ming said that by the time Aussie girls graduated from high school there were no virgins left, and by the time they went to university they were experimenting with sex toys and threesomes. Andy wasn't sure how Ming knew all this. On the rare occasions Andy had asked him, Ming had waved his hands and said, 'It's well known,' which made Andy feel stupid.

At ten-thirty his phone beeped on the bedside table. He picked it up and saw a message from his aunt.

How are things at the old lady's house?

Winnie was the only one in his family who messaged him in English. Andy looked around at the stained carpet and the bookcase full of books with faded yellow spines.

It's good, he typed. He didn't want his aunt to worry.

Great! See what a genius your Auntie Winnie is? If only your Uncle Craig appreciated this!

Andy sent her a smiley-face emoji.

His aunt sent three blowing-kiss emojis back.

Andy put his phone on the bedside table and picked his microbiology textbook up from the floor. He had an exam worth thirty per cent in eight weeks and he'd barely studied for it. The pink cells and eggplant-coloured bacteria in the photographs reminded him of Mrs Hughes' quilt, the one he'd buried beneath the bed. The book informed him that the 'lancet-shaped, gram-positive bacteria' were actually *Streptococcus pneumoniae*, a dangerous pathogen responsible for ear infections and pneumonia. Andy found it hard to believe that these tiny dots—which during his first prac he'd mistaken for dust on the microscope lens—could kill people. In fact, he found most things he studied in biomedicine a little hard to fathom. Things like neuroplasticity and phantom limbs and auditory hallucinations. It all felt more like magic than medicine. Ever since he was a child, Andy had been deeply suspicious of magicians. He envied Ming, who approached each new topic with a clear and open mind—like a child, innocent and trusting.

Andy studied three pages before dropping the book to the floor. As he turned off the light he remembered how, before retiring to bed, Mrs Hughes had thrown a blanket over Atticus's cage. She'd said the darkness simulated night-time and helped anxious birds to sleep. Andy had felt jealous of Atticus then. He wished someone would smother the endless chatter of his brain with a big black sheet.

5

When Meg woke up, she felt refreshed. In the mirror, her cheeks looked less jowly and the bags around her eyes were not so grey. She briefly considered applying some lipstick before breakfast but then scolded herself for her vanity—young people like Andy didn't care how an old woman like her looked. She was invisible, whether she wore lipstick or not. She closed the zip on her make-up bag and ran a comb through her hair.

When she got to the kitchen she found Andy sitting at the breakfast table, staring into his coffee.

'Good morning!' she said, which seemed to startle him. 'How did you sleep?'

He shook his head. 'All night there was a banging noise on the roof.'

'That would've been the possums,' Meg said. 'Do you know about possums?'

'In possum land the nights are fair!' Atticus sang from his cage. Meg removed the cover and stuck a finger through the bars. The parrot bit down on her knuckle with his beak.

'I don't think it was an animal,' the boy said. He looked wretched. 'It was too big to be a possum.'

'Believe me, it was a possum,' Meg insisted. She put two pieces of bread in the toaster. 'Would you like some breakfast?'

Andy glanced at Meg and then at Atticus. 'No thank you.'

She filled the kettle from the tap. 'My friend Jill is picking me up this morning. We go for coffee every Wednesday.'

'Okay.' Andy took off his glasses and rubbed his face vigorously with his hand. 'I have uni.'

'Oh, good.' The toaster beeped and Meg plucked the toast from its metal grills. 'Don't forget to lock the door on your way out.'

Andy stood up. 'Do you mind if I take a shower?'

'Go right ahead.'

As Andy left the kitchen, Meg wondered what Jillian would make of her new housemate. She would probably say he was a typical millennial—rude, self-absorbed, brittle. Jillian was constantly bemoaning millennials, but Meg didn't believe people fitted neatly into categories. She was supposed to be a baby boomer, but she wasn't a fat cat like Jillian with lots of investment properties. She didn't have a book club or go on luxury holidays like their friend Anne. Perhaps Andy was the same. An outlier.

Andy emerged from the bathroom just as Jillian arrived. He had a towel wrapped around his waist and was clutching his pyjamas to his chest. On seeing the women, he scurried to his bedroom and closed the door behind him. Meg grabbed her jacket from the hatstand in the hallway.

'Let's go,' she said, avoiding Jillian's suggestive smile.

Every Wednesday Meg, Jillian and Anne drank coffee at Café Bonjour, a small place next to the chemist along Meg's local shopping strip. Jillian and Anne both lived on the other side of the city, but unlike Meg they still owned cars and could make the trip across town.

The manager of the café was a Vietnamese woman who played Edith Piaf on a loop and served baguettes stuffed with chillies. Meg liked the coffee, but she couldn't eat the baguettes. The one time she'd tried, the crust had shredded the skin on the roof of her mouth and she hadn't been able to eat anything, other than yoghurt, for days. The suburb had changed so much since she and Jillian were kids, back when they could buy sixpence-worth of their favourite lollies— freckles and snakes—from the milk bar. Now the main street boasted an organic food store, a nail salon and a pilates studio with a terrible name: Keeping Karm. Every week Anne declared how much the suburb had *evolved*—as if, rather than a postcode, it was some kind of living, breathing organism.

Anne was already there when they arrived, reading the newspaper on her iPad. She was a self-confessed iPad addict, which intrigued Meg, who couldn't get her head around how

26

to use a smart phone. But Meg was impressed by the way her friend's arthritic fingers danced across the small screen—here, a photomontage of her five grandchildren; there, the latest article from the *New Yorker*.

'Ladies!' Anne said when she spotted her friends.

Meg braced herself for the next hour and a half, which would be less a conversation and more a competition between Anne and Jillian for centre stage. Meg missed the days when it had just been her and Jill. They'd been unlikely friends since the age of five and had endured so much together—Helen's accident, relationship break-ups, losing their parents—and even though Jillian had left to live in places like Sydney and London, it was never long before she returned to their little suburb, first for weddings and the births of her grandchildren, and later to care for her dying mother.

The weekly coffees had started at Jillian's insistence after Helen had passed away. In spite of Meg's initial reluctance—she hadn't wanted to monopolise Jillian's time, she always seemed so busy—the catch-ups had been a welcome distraction. That was three years ago. Now they hardly ever spoke of Helen. Instead they talked about books and Jillian's children and how long Meg had been waiting for her knee replacement in the public health system. What had begun as therapy had morphed into a kind of habit. Often Meg wondered if Jillian felt sorry for her. Though her friend liked to paint herself as tough—one of the original feminists, who'd only married to relieve her lovesick husband of his suffering—in truth, she had a gentle heart. But she was also easily bored, and Meg wasn't surprised when one day Jillian suggested they search Facebook for old high school friends. Meg had agreed—she couldn't bear to see Jillian restless—but she was disappointed.

Meg wasn't on Facebook, so Jillian did all the work. She reported back that some of their classmates had moved interstate and quite a few had died. They both took delight in the discovery that bitchy Robyn—who'd been blessed (or cursed) with huge breasts in first form—had been married and divorced four times. The only person Jillian had found who wasn't awful and still lived in Melbourne was Anne 'Hound Dog' Harris. Robyn had given Anne the nickname after discovering her one afternoon in the school toilets, bawling her eyes out about a boy. From that day on, when the nuns were out of earshot, Robyn would point to Anne, make her best Elvis face and sing the chorus of 'Hound Dog'. Anne would sit at her desk, steely-faced, and silently endure Robyn's torments, but it must have had an effect on her, because by the time they all reached fourth form, nothing seemed to touch her. Even the nuns, sensing her fearlessness, treated her with a special respect.

At their reunion, Meg was thrilled to discover that Anne had lost none of her steel. Everything about her, from her sharp-edged earrings to her patent-leather heels, was unapologetic and bold. Anne told them she now ran a high-end clothing boutique.

'I've ordered for you, Meg,' Anne declared when the women sat down. 'But Jill's order is always so complicated with her skinny this and decaf that, I figured she could do it herself.' As she spoke, her oversized red hoop earrings jiggled and bounced. In spite of the twenty-degree day, she was draped in a shaggy, mustard-coloured shawl.

The waitress, a timid girl with smudged eyeliner and a French accent, arrived with the two coffees. She took Jillian's order.

'Just an extra-hot skinny decaf latte for me,' Jillian said.

'See?' Anne picked up her coffee before putting it straight down again with a clatter. She shook her fingers and inhaled through gritted teeth. 'Why do they insist on serving hot drinks in a glass?' She frowned and wrapped a serviette around the tumbler.

Meg saw the young couple at the table next to them snigger.

Oblivious, Anne continued. 'So, ladies, I have news.' She paused, making sure she had their full attention. 'I have a new companion.'

Meg felt her heart hammer—was Anne mocking her? Did she know about Andy? But then she saw Anne hold up her iPad. On the screen was a photo of a scrawny-looking kitten.

'A stray I rescued. I've named her Miss Marmalade.'

'She's lovely,' Meg cooed, relieved, and passed the iPad to Jillian.

'You should get one. They're easy to care for,' Anne said. 'So long as you don't have allergies to them.'

'I'm not sure Atticus would approve,' Meg said, taking a sip of her coffee.

'Oh, yes, I forgot about that.'

'Speaking of companions,' Jillian said, and nudged Meg beneath the table. 'I snatched a glimpse of *your* new housemate coming out of the shower this morning.'

Anne put her coffee down. 'New housemate? You didn't tell me about this.'

Meg studied the elaborate leaf design the barista had fashioned in the foam on her cappuccino. Anything was better than looking into the interrogating eyes of her two friends. Sometimes, with their pointy faces and feathery shawls, they reminded Meg of a couple of vultures.

'Is he Chinese?' Jillian said, and Meg saw the couple at the next table giggle some more.

'Shhhh.' Meg held a finger to her lips.

'Oooh!' Anne said, clapping her hands. 'Now I *am* interested.'

Meg explained the homeshare arrangement to Anne. Jillian knew all about it, despite her feigned ignorance. It was Jillian who had brought home the brochure from the library, setting the whole thing in motion.

'What a wonderful idea,' Anne said, and Meg thought she seemed genuine. 'I guess it must get lonely, and scary, with everything that's happened.'

Meg shrugged, keen to avoid talk of the intruder.

'What's he like?' Jillian said in such a salacious tone that Meg felt her cheeks flush.

'He keeps to himself.'

'Studious, I imagine,' Anne said. 'They always are.'

'Anne!' Jillian exclaimed, but she was smiling.

Meg looked over at the amused couple sitting beside them. She took another sip of her coffee. 'I don't actually know what he studies.'

'Medicine, I bet,' Anne offered.

Jillian slapped the back of Anne's hand. 'I hope he's a contemporary dancer, just to prove you wrong.'

Meg licked the froth from her lips. 'I'll ask him.'

6

It was ten am and Andy was on the tram, studying photos of possums on his smart phone. He couldn't believe one of those pink-nosed creatures was responsible for keeping him up all night, and yet he found numerous online forums devoted to discussing their roof-surfing habits. Some people suggested traps, while others swore by aluminium skirts wrapped around neighbouring trees. Andy even stumbled across the poem Atticus had quoted from that morning—'In Possum Land'—written by a famous Australian poet, Henry Lawson.

Ming was waiting for him at the tram stop next to the medical building. His friend was hunched over his phone and didn't see Andy arrive. He flicked Ming on the ear.

'Hey!' Ming said, pulling out his earbuds. 'You're late.'

He hitched his bag onto his shoulder and they walked to the laboratory together. 'Man, where were you last night? I sent you three messages about going for wonton noodles.'

Andy had seen Ming's texts, but they'd only depressed him—an unwelcome reminder of how far he was from the city.

'My phone was on silent,' he lied. 'Anyway, now it takes me thirty-five minutes on the tram to get to Chinatown.'

Ming huffed. 'I don't know what you're thinking, staying with an old woman in the middle of nowhere. I told you a thousand times you're welcome to crash on my sofa bed.'

Andy had been tempted by his friend's offer, but he knew that Ming suffered from severe obsessive-compulsive disorder, and during swot vac he spent entire days locked in his apartment, washing his hands. Luckily Ming was smart and studied consistently the rest of the year.

'Mum and Dad wouldn't accept it,' Andy said, knowing his friend would stop probing when he heard parents were involved. He and Ming were both from Hong Kong, and both only children—if there was one thing Ming understood, it was the irrational and unquestionable authority of family.

'So, what's it like?' Ming asked.

Andy thought of the dark corridors and the dust and the rodents on the roof. 'Horrible.'

'How old is she?'

Andy frowned. 'Seventies, eighties? I don't know—it's hard to tell.'

'Australians always look older than they are,' Ming said. 'My mum says it's the hole in the ozone layer—the sun's too strong for their skin.'

Andy cleared his throat. 'She's got a pet parrot.'

'Seriously?'

'Yeah, an African grey something called Atticus. He's nearly thirty, older than us.'

'No way.'

'I swear. It's crazy. This morning he was reciting poetry.'

Ming put his hand on Andy's arm, his black eyes glistening. 'You should teach it Cantonese. Get it to say some Confucius.'

Andy had hoped to impress his friend but, as usual, Ming was making a joke of it.

'I don't know any Confucius.'

Ming stopped to think. 'Neither do I.'

During microbiology prac, Andy copied Ming's answers. He found the Latin names of the bacteria impossible to commit to memory. *Streptococcus, enterococcus, haemophilus*—they all sounded the same to him. A little like Australian names when he'd first arrived in Melbourne—Laura and Lauren, Daniel and Danielle, Christine and Christopher. It was confusing.

As the tutor wandered around the lab, peering over students' shoulders, Andy watched Kiko—a half-Japanese, half-Australian girl who sat at the bench opposite him. Andy had spent countless hours sketching her and studying her movements. He felt like he knew her intimately, even though they'd never exchanged a word. Sometimes, when he was at the library, he would watch her through the floor-to-ceiling windows. She always sat on the lawn near the law building to eat lunch with her best friend, Muneera. While Kiko kept to herself, everybody in biomedicine knew Muneera. In tutorials, she answered questions in an urgent, explosive way, as if she was on a game show and a lot of money was at stake. Kiko seemed content to remain in Muneera's shadow, which amazed Andy, but not as much as the fact that Kiko—and indeed the whole world—seemed completely unaware of Kiko's beauty. Perhaps it was because she wore shapeless jeans and never applied make-up. But such things didn't bother Andy—if anything, they endeared her to him. In Andy's mind, Kiko was perfect. Even at a distance, through the library's unwashed window, her glossy hair and fleeting smiles were a welcome relief from the schematic diagrams of polymerase chain reactions. Andy's notebook was full of drawings—of the back of Kiko's head, of the perfect U made by her earlobe, of her big brown eyes with their long black lashes.

The tutor asked Kiko if he could take a look through her microscope. Andy watched the lanky scientist lean over to adjust the focus of the lens. He was inches from her. Andy wondered what she smelled like—something citrusy, he imagined, something like freshly peeled mandarins. As the tutor examined the slide, Kiko studied her fingernails. She bit a sliver of nail and looked up, self-conscious. Andy peered into his microscope, pretending to be fascinated by the pseudohyphae of a fungus.

7

At dinner the next night, Meg asked Andy what he was studying.

'Biomedicine,' he said through a mouthful of mashed potato.

'Is that a science degree?'

Andy swallowed. 'Pretty much. It's a three-year science degree with a focus on medical subjects.'

Meg suppressed a sigh. She would've loved to prove Anne wrong—wiped some of the arrogance from her perfectly made-up face. But if Meg looked disappointed, Andy didn't notice. In fact, nothing much seemed to register with Meg's new housemate. In the three days they'd lived together, she could count on one hand the number of times he'd made eye contact.

She watched him now, pushing a piece of steak around his plate with his fork. That morning she'd walked all the way to the butcher, and now her knees were throbbing beneath the table. She'd spent fifteen dollars of her pension on the meat, only to have Andy spit the half-chewed chunks into his napkin.

'Perhaps once a week you could do the shopping and buy some things, like noodles, for yourself.'

'Okay,' Andy said, pushing back his chair. He picked up his plate with its rearranged but otherwise untouched food.

'I want you to feel at home here,' Meg said. 'My house is your house, that sort of thing.'

'Thank you.'

'I mean it.' Meg leant back and curled a finger around one of the bars of Atticus's cage. 'Invite a friend over. Anything.'

The parrot jumped from his swing to perch on the bars of the cage. Meg scratched the back of his neck.

'Fine and dandy. Sugar candy!' Atticus sang.

As soon as dinner was finished, Andy retreated to his room. Meg sat in the lounge, alone, watching *The Voice*. When Meg had applied to the homeshare program, she'd been seeking the protection of an extra body—preferably male—inside her house. She'd hoped for somebody quiet, somebody who kept to himself. She'd said as much to the skinny lady with kind eyes at the homeshare office. But now Meg wondered if perhaps she wanted more than that—some company, a snippet of conversation, some remedy for the loneliness she'd felt since Helen had passed away. And while she'd slept more soundly these past few nights knowing Andy was in the next room, now she found herself scrutinising their interactions. Why didn't he make eye contact? Did he hate her? What did he do for all those hours, locked away in his room?

Meg had travelled briefly in her thirties, before her father died. She'd even stopped over in Hong Kong, where Andy was from, on her way to London to visit her aunt. But that was a long time ago. The glimmering metropolis she saw nowadays on TV was unfamiliar. All she could really remember was the smell—a mixture of rotting vegetables and dead animals and sewage—that had flooded the plane like mustard gas as they landed at Kai Tak airport, and the rage she'd felt on returning to the hotel to discover she'd been pickpocketed—her wallet missing and the bottom of her handbag slashed open like the belly of a fish.

Meg decided against sharing such stories with Andy. She didn't want him to think that the only recollections she had of his home were bad smells and petty crime. If anything, having Andy in the house made her realise how little she knew about the world. Her universe, after her parents had passed away, had been the family home and Helen. For years Meg had listened to Anne and Jillian speak of Paris and Rome without so much as a twinge of envy, and yet now, with the arrival of this quiet student from Hong Kong, she felt a burning curiosity about the world.

Meg sat up in her recliner, found her slippers with her feet. She turned off the TV. She hadn't really been watching it. These days everything was reality television, but the shows were unlike any reality Meg had ever experienced—home cooks creating masterpieces from gold leaves and salted caramel, people losing two-thirds of their body weight as a woman with a fake tan yelled at them, D-grade celebrities agreeing to live together in a house with no walls and cameras in the bathrooms. What ever happened to *Bandstand* and *I Love Lucy*? Those were the shows she and Helen had watched as teenagers, but they seemed tame and simple by current standards. Meg supposed they couldn't go back to that age of innocence. Not after all the revelations about celebrities like Bill Cosby and Rolf Harris. She supposed they were stuck with people kissing in swimming pools and crying into their tiramisu. Meg accepted this. She only wished they would all do it a little more quietly. Nobody valued silence anymore—if anything, they seemed unnerved by it. She was shocked when she saw young students, Andy's age, walking around with headphones the size of earmuffs clamped to their temples— unaware if the birds were chirping or the leaves were rustling or a truck was hurtling towards them.

Meg turned off the lamp and made her way across the dark room to the hall. Outside Andy's room, she stopped and listened for the creak of a floorboard, the groan of a mattress spring, a snore, but there was nothing. As she walked the short distance to her bedroom, she felt acutely aware of her heavy, hippo-like movements—the beams of the house seeming to crackle like dry kindling around her. When Andy moved out, Meg wondered, would he leave a trace? Or would his presence be as ghostly as a breeze wafting through the dusty hallway?

8

Andy was lying on his bed, glowering at his laptop. He was studying his academic transcript from first semester. The last thing he wanted to do after the collapse of his father's cleaning business was to create more stress for his parents by failing his second year of university. In the first few weeks of the semester, fresh from the holidays, Andy had been feeling upbeat, but as assignment deadlines loomed and the exams crept closer, his earlier optimism disappeared.

Last week, he'd broken down during a meeting with the course coordinator. The coordinator had been so concerned, she'd organised an urgent appointment with the counsellor. For an hour a woman with polka-dot stockings and dangly earrings had asked Andy about his feelings. She'd interrogated him about how he felt about everything from being separated from his family to the changeable weather in Melbourne. She'd taught him a couple of relaxation techniques, which Andy had found helpful, but he couldn't understand how spending an hour a week explaining his feelings was going to help him pass his exams. If anything, it was one hour less spent studying—maybe more, if he considered the time required to get to the appointment plus the minutes waiting for her to finish with the student before him. For most of the session, Andy stared at the infinity tattoo on the counsellor's wrist, tracing its curves with his eyes, over and over.

He kept thinking back to what Ming had said about paying somebody to sit his exams for him. Apparently such a service existed—run by an extensive underground network of ex-students. 'I swear,' Ming said as he slapped Andy on the back, 'we could get a Vietnamese girl to sit your neuroscience exam and nobody would know the difference.' Andy couldn't tell if Ming was joking. It was easy for him—he was smart and knew how to study. He had good genes too—his dad was a neurosurgeon and his mum was a cardiologist. His only impediment was his OCD, and even that seemed to work in his favour. It made him obsess about nitty-gritty details like which three bacteria most commonly caused meningitis in neonates—the perfect skill for acing exams. Sometimes Andy wondered why Ming was even friends with him. The only conclusion that made any sense was that he found Andy entertaining. Perhaps watching Andy fail was as compelling as a Korean soap opera, or a five-car pile-up on the freeway.

Andy agreed with Ming's prediction that nobody in the

exam room would notice if someone else was in his seat. The classes were so big and so much of the content was administered online, it was hard for students to keep track of their classmates. Not to mention that on exam day everyone was so focused on themselves and their palpitating hearts, they wouldn't pay attention to one extra stranger. Especially not a quiet, bespectacled Asian stranger.

Andy chewed his thumbnail. He'd never been a great student. He'd always had to work longer and harder to do as well as his cousin, Wei, who'd been in the same class as him at school in Hong Kong—his smarter and better-looking cousin, or so all the teachers said.

Andy snapped the lid of his laptop shut and pulled his notebook from his backpack. He looked at the drawings of Kiko scattered amid all the diagrams of the optic chiasm. His eyes lingered on a sketch of her profile. The nose was wrong, but he felt a swell of pride at the pleasing curve of her hair and the perfect arc of her ear.

9

They settled into a routine quickly. Meg woke early, sometime between six and seven. She drank a cup of English breakfast tea and ate two pieces of marmalade toast before washing her mug and plate and leaving them to dry in the dish rack. While she showered and dressed for the day, Andy made a cup of instant coffee in the kitchen. He left his mug—a Pfizer one, advertising Viagra—unwashed in the sink. He didn't eat breakfast. As Meg moved around the house, spraying the few house plants in the lounge room with water, Andy got dressed.

Occasionally, when Meg had sat down in the lounge to rest her legs and read a few pages of her book, she would catch a glimpse of Andy before he left for the day. He was always in a rush—to leave the table, to go back to his room, to get away from her and the house. A few times she had yelled goodbye, only to be answered by the slam of the front door.

While he was out, Meg followed the sun around the house like a cat. She spent the morning in the east-facing lounge room and the afternoon on the back verandah. It was the start of spring, and she enjoyed spotting new eruptions of colour amid the leafy mess of the backyard. The jacaranda wouldn't bloom until late November, but even its empty branches looked majestic in the afternoon light.

Sometime around five o'clock, the smack of the flyscreen door would rouse Meg from her nap on the back porch and she'd move inside to make a start on dinner. Meg hadn't minded cooking so much when she was doing it for Helen, but living on her own she'd come to loathe it. After Helen's death, Meg had often settled for a bowl of stale cereal with long-life milk, or skipped dinner altogether. Nowadays she spent a good ten minutes trying to decide whether to defrost some bolognese sauce or throw a handful of fish fingers into the oven. She supposed it was better this way—at least her body got a bit of protein. But she wondered how long she could keep it up. Andy hadn't mentioned the ten hours of weekly service and Meg hadn't had the guts to bring it up again. She could tell from the nervous way he moved around the kitchen that he'd never cooked for himself. The only things he'd contributed to the pantry so far were a cardboard box of Cup Noodles, three KitKats and a jar of instant coffee.

Tonight she made a salad from some leftover pasta and a can of tuna. She popped two pieces of frozen bread into the toaster. As she dished the salad into bowls, Andy entered the kitchen. He pulled a glass tumbler down from the cupboard and filled it with tap water.

'How was your day?' Meg said, knowing immediately it was the wrong thing to say—too much like a wife greeting her husband after a long day at work.

Andy drank the water greedily. 'It was okay,' he said when he'd finished. He put his empty glass in the sink.

Meg would have to tell him to start washing his dishes, but not today. 'I've made a pasta salad,' she said as she buttered the toast.

Andy sat down at the table. 'Thank you.'

Meg placed the bowl of salad in front of him and watched him take a bite.

'It's cold,' he said, spitting the penne into a serviette.

'It's a salad.'

Andy ate the toast instead.

'Do you eat salads in Hong Kong?'

'A few dishes are served cold. Chicken. Pickles. Jellyfish.'

'Jellyfish?'

'Yes, but we only eat that as an appetiser, when we go out to restaurants.'

For a minute nobody spoke. Atticus sang the alphabet song from his cage.

'So you've eaten jellyfish but you've never had a pasta salad?' Meg said.

'Yes.'

She was about to apologise but stopped herself. She filled her mouth with pasta instead. As much as she hated to admit it, the salad was horribly bland. There was no colour or texture or spice—she might as well have been eating cardboard. Andy's Cup Noodles with all their MSG almost certainly had more flavour. But it had been decades since Meg had derived pleasure from eating. For her, meals were a chore, like showering or brushing her teeth. Necessary but boring.

Andy finished his toast and excused himself. He scrubbed the crumbs from his bread plate and left it to dry in the dish rack. It was the first time Meg had seen him clean up. When he was gone, she ate her dinner slowly, one piece of cold pasta at a time. She stared at Andy's bowl of untouched food, his empty chair.

10

It was mid-semester break, exactly five weeks until swot vac. This thought was enough to keep Andy up at night. When he turned on the light and tried to study, his eyes burned and blurred with fatigue, but as soon as he lay down in the dark again, his mind raced as if he was on speed. Thoughts flooded his brain at such a rapid pace he struggled to keep up. Giant rod-shaped bacteria. Neurons like exploding meteorites. His mother, beating him with the feather duster; his father, flinching with each stroke. Every so often a moment of reprieve—a flash of Kiko, her long fingers, her shiny hair, her reluctant, soft-lipped smile.

At three am Andy heard the bang of a possum landing on the roof. Exasperated, he got up. It was like living in a haunted house. As he crept down the hall in his slippers he avoided looking at the framed photographs on the wall. He knew the people in the pictures were dead. They'd probably died inside the house. This didn't bother Andy—in his grandmother's flat, there'd been a black and white photo of Andy's great-grandfather, together with an urn containing his ashes, on a shelf above the kitchen sink. But there was something about number four Rose Street, a sadness Andy felt as soon as he stepped through the front door.

A gentle glow emanated from the kitchen. Perhaps the old lady had left a light on by mistake. Andy was surprised to find Mrs Hughes sitting at the table in her dressing-gown, nursing a cup of tea. She'd lit a candle instead of turning on the ceiling light, presumably to avoid waking the parrot. Her face was a puzzle of shadows.

'Possums?' she said, and for a moment Andy wondered if he was talking to a ghost.

He nodded. 'You too?'

Mrs Hughes shook her head. 'I'm not afraid of possums. I'm a chronic insomniac.' She took a sip of her tea. 'I'm afraid of my dreams.'

Andy smiled, unsure if this was a joke.

Mrs Hughes moved to stand up. 'Can I make you a cup of tea?'

'No, please, sit down.' He felt bad that she was always doing things for him. He hadn't forgotten about the ten hours of housework he was supposed to do. Andy wished he knew about cooking or gardening. He was terrified Mrs Hughes might ask him to clean the bathroom, which was in desperate need of a good scrub. Every night before he showered, Andy removed his glasses, thankful he wouldn't have to see all the mould in the grout as he washed himself. But the thought of getting down on his hands and knees with a brush and actually touching the stuff made him shudder. He grabbed two Cup Noodles from the pantry and flicked the switch on the kettle. 'Would you like one?'

Mrs Hughes eyed the cup in Andy's hands.

'It's really nice if you crack an egg into it,' he told her.

'Okay,' she said, 'I'm feeling peckish.'

Andy enjoyed being able to do something for his host. He poured boiling water into the paper cups and stirred them with a fork for two minutes. Mrs Hughes fetched the eggs from the fridge and watched him crack one into each cup before stirring some more. When he placed the steaming soup noodles in front of the old lady, she inhaled deeply through her nose.

'It's good,' she said, after taking a sip.

'Not bad.'

'A little spicy.'

'Yes.'

They went back to slurping their soup. When Andy had finished eating all the noodles, he drank the remaining liquid straight from the paper cup. Mrs Hughes watched him.

'It's the best way,' Andy said.

She lifted the cup to her lips. When she had finished she wiped her mouth on her sleeve. 'The perfect midnight snack.'

They heard a light purring noise from Atticus's cage.

'At least somebody's sleeping,' Mrs Hughes said, and laughed.

OCTOBER

11

It was Wednesday. Andy had already left for uni and Jillian was late. As she waited, Meg peered through the curtains of the lounge room window at the pearly buds on the ornamental pear tree.

They'd taken a two-week break from their weekly coffees because Jillian had been away. Meg and Anne didn't meet up without Jillian—they'd tried once and it had been awkward and unpleasant. Meg knew that much of Anne's performance was for Jillian's benefit anyway—friendly but competitive banter. Without her, Anne was impatient, occasionally even a little bitchy. In truth, Meg didn't mind a break from the routine—she was dreading Anne's I-told-you-so smile when she found out Andy was studying biomedicine.

Meg knew something was wrong as soon as she saw Jillian stumble up the driveway. She rushed to the door and opened it before her friend had a chance to knock. Instead of saying hello, Jillian walked straight past her towards the lounge room.

'What's happened? Is Henry okay?' Meg asked. Henry was Jillian's husband. He had diabetes and was always being admitted to hospital.

'No.' Jillian pulled a ball of tissue from her pocket. She squeezed it in her hand. 'It's Anne.'

Meg sat down on the couch. Anne was never unwell.

'Her heart, apparently,' Jillian said and dabbed her nose with the ball of tissue. White flakes fell like snow onto the carpet. 'Last week she told me she'd need a lift to the café today. She was planning to take her car in for a service. But when I arrived to pick her up I found Greg sitting on the verandah. He was still wearing his pyjamas. She died three days ago.'

'My God.' Meg felt the hair on her forearms stand on end.

'In the middle of pilates. She excused herself from the class and collapsed in the gym stairwell.'

'Christ.'

'Greg said she'd been complaining of indigestion, but she'd refused to see a doctor.' A drop of snot snaked down from Jillian's nostril to her top lip. 'He felt terribly guilty, the poor man.'

'She was so stubborn,' Meg said without thinking, and immediately felt bad for speaking ill of the dead.

In spite of the heat, Jillian shivered. While she'd been waiting, Meg had drawn the curtains and turned off the lights in the lounge room. It felt wrong now, in the face of tragedy, to deal with trivial things like lighting. They sat like statues in the dark.

'Would a cup of tea help?' Meg said after several minutes had passed.

Jillian nodded. 'We won't be going to the café today.'

'Of course not.'

'Not for a while.'

Meg sat down at the kitchen table while she waited for the water to boil. She'd lost people before, but she had always expected to outlive her family—her mother and father were old and Helen had been ill for a long time. She hadn't expected to outlive Anne. From her friend's despondent state in the lounge room, Meg guessed Jillian felt the same way.

The kettle boiled and Meg prepared the tea. It was at times like these that formalities seemed particularly important. She arranged the teacups and sugar bowl on a silver tray. When she returned to the lounge room, Jillian had regained some of her colour.

Jillian took the tea gratefully, resting the hot cup in her lap. 'Anne was such a pain in the arse sometimes, but such great fun too.'

'Yes,' Meg agreed. She knew they had to partake in this messy ritual of weepy nostalgia, but she felt weary at the prospect of it.

'The funeral is this Friday.'

Meg hadn't been to a funeral in years. She supposed that was one good thing about not having many friends. 'Where?' she asked.

'At their local church. Anne would have hated it, but Greg and the kids insisted.'

This surprised Meg. Anne had always been scathing about religion. She'd hated the nuns at their Catholic school with a special savagery, which had made her something of a hero in sixth form. Meg and Jill drank the rest of their tea to the sound of Atticus singing and squawking in the kitchen.

'I'll give you a lift,' Jillian said, returning her cup to its saucer. 'I'll drop by around twelve.'

'If it's not too much trouble.'

Jillian stood up. She wrapped her silk scarf around her neck. 'Just don't die on me.'

12

Andy came home to an empty lounge room and a note waiting for him on the kitchen table. *Help yourself to the spaghetti. I've gone to bed with a headache.* Andy had only been living with Mrs Hughes for three weeks, but she'd already cooked spaghetti bolognese on at least ten occasions. Andy scooped a portion of the refrigerated pasta into the bin to make it look as if he'd eaten it, and then cracked an egg into some Cup Noodles.

'Hot potato!' Atticus screeched.

'Not potato, *noodles*,' Andy corrected him. 'Can you say *noodles*?'

'Can you say noodles?' the bird replied.

Andy remembered what Mrs Hughes had said about the

parrot mocking her. He bowed his head and ate his dinner.
Bored, Atticus turned his attention to a bottle cap on the floor
of his cage.

At ten past five Andy's phone rang.

'Hello?'

'Have you eaten yet?' Andy's father asked. A standard
Cantonese greeting.

'Yes,' Andy replied, throwing his empty noodle cup in the
rubbish bin. It was usually his mum who called, during her
lunchbreak, which was around midafternoon in Melbourne.
'Is something the matter?' He could hear the bustle of Hong
Kong in the background—the hiss of a bus door, the beeping
of pedestrian lights, the shudder of a jackhammer.

'It's your mother.'

Andy didn't need to hear more. The illness that had
plagued her all his life had returned again, he knew it. The
last time was when he was fifteen—seven long and medicated
years ago. Andy's memories of that time were sketchy, mostly
because they never spoke of it. Every day, for a week, Andy
had been left with his grandparents in their tiny flat in Tai
Koo Shing. As his mother lay sedated somewhere on the other
side of the island, Andy and his grandmother had watched
Cantonese soap operas—hypnotised by the men with long
plaits seducing women with powdered faces. Sometimes he'd
daydreamt about himself soaring, swords drawn and robes
flapping, across cloudless skies. He remembered his father
returning late in the afternoon, rubbing his tired eyes.

Atticus whistled a tune in his cage.

'What's that noise?' Andy's father asked.

'Nothing. What's happened to Mum?'

'She's gone to hospital. For a rest.'

This was how his father spoke—in a series of soothing euphemisms. His mother had been *overworked* when they found her, floppy as a rag doll and cold as a fish, on the tiled floor of the shower. She'd been *stressed* when they'd discovered her in the kitchen smashing a frying pan at a giant snake that only she could see.

'When?' Andy asked.

'A week ago.'

Andy wasn't surprised by how long it had taken his father to tell him. In his family everything was a secret until it became impossible to hide any longer.

'Shall I come home?' Andy asked, but it was an empty offer—he knew his father would decline.

'You need to study.'

'How long will she be in hospital?'

'Not long.'

That could mean a couple of days or forever.

'The best thing you can do is to work hard. Get high enough marks to get into medicine.'

'Yes, Dad.'

Perhaps his father sensed his helplessness, because his voice took on a chirpier tone. 'It's your birthday soon.'

Andy had forgotten all about it. He would be turning twenty-two on Friday.

'Your mother and I have transferred two thousand dollars to your account. That's lai see from your aunts and uncles as well as us. You should thank them. Spend a little and save the rest. Take your friends out to dinner, do something nice.'

Such generosity was unheard of. His mother must be really sick. Andy thanked his father and hung up the phone. He looked through the window past the trees towards the haemorrhaging sun.

That night, Andy searched the internet for people willing to sit his exams for him. He was astonished by the number of websites devoted to cheating at university, and even more so by how openly they advertised their services. He eventually found someone called Kanbei who had taken the same biomedicine course and graduated with honours—or so he claimed—three years ago. Through a series of text messages they arranged to meet at a Chinese takeaway place on Friday. When it was done, Andy plugged his phone into the charger beside his bed. Rather than feeling nervous about the pending encounter, he felt relieved. He opened the door to his room and used his hands to find his way down the dark hall to the kitchen. He was both thirsty and a little hungry, and he'd spied a packet of Tim Tams in the cupboard earlier that day. As he walked past Mrs Hughes' room he paused. There was an odd noise coming through the door. It sounded like an animal whimpering—something smaller and more timid than a possum. As he moved, a loose floorboard announced his presence with a creak. The whimpering stopped. Andy held his breath. He counted to three and tiptoed the rest of the way to the kitchen. It was only once he was munching on a biscuit that he recognised the noise for what it was— Mrs Hughes weeping.

13

Meg had been given Andy's personal details with his application—his previous address on Spencer Street, his next of kin, his passport number. She wasn't sure what had made her look at the paperwork again, but she was glad she had, because otherwise she would have completely missed his birthday.

Anne's funeral was that afternoon and Meg was in search of a distraction. She decided to bake Andy something for his birthday—her mother's famous pineapple upside-down cake. She was certain she had all the ingredients she needed— brown sugar, flour, butter, eggs, milk, tinned pineapple—so she wouldn't need to go to the shops. She'd been hoping Andy might do a weekly trip to the supermarket, but since their Cup Noodles midnight snack, Meg had hardly seen him. Recently she'd had to resort to communicating with him through post-it notes stuck to the fridge. She supposed she could take it up with the agency, but she didn't want to get Andy in trouble. She reminded herself that he was always home at a reasonable hour, and that he was quiet, and tidy.

She got to work on the cake. It felt good to bake again, to melt butter and sugar and feel the warmth of the oven on her legs. She normally scoffed at cooking shows like *MasterChef*, but today she appreciated the therapeutic power of creating something to eat, especially something rich and sticky, from a pile of nothing.

As the cake baked, Meg got dressed for the funeral. She opened her wardrobe and picked out a black blouse and a pair of pleated black slacks. She put on the earrings she'd worn to Helen's memorial—the pearl drops her mother had left her in her will. As a tribute to Anne, she added one of Helen's brooches to the ensemble—a gold kitten with a ruby bow and diamante eyes.

The doorbell rang just as Meg was pulling the cake out of the oven. She placed it on a wire rack on the stovetop and hung her oven mitt on a hook beside the rangehood. When she turned around, Jillian was standing in the kitchen.

'The front door was open,' Jillian said as they kissed.

'Andy must've forgotten to lock it.'

'I thought this boy was supposed to look after your safety, not put you at greater risk.'

Jillian was wearing a black dress with black lace sleeves. She hadn't bothered with eyeliner or mascara and was as pale as a ghost. 'You've been baking?' she said.

'It was something to do.'

'I know the feeling. This morning I weeded the garden and scrubbed the grout in all the bathrooms.' Jillian wiped her nose with a handkerchief from her pocket. 'Anne would've preferred the baking.'

Meg smiled. She pointed to the brooch.

Jillian cooed. 'Miss Marmalade.'

Meg's thoughts turned to the stray Anne had rescued from the skip. 'What will happen to her now?'

'I don't know. Greg hates cats.'

'She'd be a constant reminder.'

'Maybe I'll take her in.'

'Really?' Meg was surprised. Jillian was not and never had been an animal person. The few times Meg had asked her to mind Atticus, she had backed away, citing allergies.

'I guess we can all do with a little companionship some-times,' Jillian said. 'Like you and your Chinese student.'

14

The fast-food place smelled of oil and ginger and spring onions. Andy sat down at a long table near the window. Kanbei had said he'd be wearing a hoodie, but it was a cold day for October and there were at least two people with hoodies in the restaurant. Andy would have to wait for Kanbei to find him. Through the window he watched a gaggle of university students chatting and laughing as they waited at the pedestrian crossing. Andy wished he could trade places with them. Perched on his stool, waiting for a stranger, foot tapping and heart hammering, he felt as if everybody had a better lot in life than him.

He couldn't believe his fifteen years of academic study had culminated in this. In Hong Kong, he may not have been a great student, but he had never come close to failing. He hadn't anticipated that the style of teaching in Australia would be so different from back home. Here the lecturers provided little to no direction at all. Sometimes Andy wondered if they were lazy. If he had to find out all the answers himself, what were his parents paying such enormous sums of money for?

His thoughts were interrupted by the screech of metal legs being dragged across the floor. He turned around to see a Chinese man in jeans and a black jumper climbing onto the stool beside him.

'Have you eaten yet?' the man asked in Cantonese.

'Not yet.'

'They do a good Hainanese chicken rice.'

'I like Hainanese chicken rice.'

Kanbei shouted their order to a man chopping roast duck behind the counter. He put his laptop on the table between them and began typing rapidly in Chinese characters.

Tap with your finger. Once for yes. Twice for no.

Andy laughed. He looked at Kanbei. 'Are you serious?'

Kanbei's glare told Andy that he was.

Are you Andy Chan? Student number 236580?

Andy hadn't given Kanbei his student number. Kanbei must have hacked into the uni database to retrieve it. There was no going back now. The realisation was equal parts suffocating and liberating. He tapped his finger on the bench.

You want me to sit your microbiology exam scheduled for Monday 19 November and your neuroscience exam scheduled for Wednesday 21 November.

Andy stared at a woman on the street who was holding a

large 'Get Well Soon' balloon. He tapped once.

You will pay $1000 per exam. $1000 now. $1000 on completion. The first amount must be transferred by close of business tomorrow to the bank account written on a piece of paper I'm going to give you now.

Andy tapped once again. He accepted the folded paper Kanbei passed him beneath the table.

No money no deal.

Outside, a couple of students were kissing, oblivious to the illicit deal being made on the other side of the window. Andy watched a thread of saliva stretch between them as the girl pulled away.

Understand?

Andy tapped yes. He cleaned his chopsticks with a napkin, the way his father did when they went to restaurants. He slipped the note with the account details into his pocket.

Kanbei held his middle finger down on the delete key of his laptop. Andy watched the Chinese characters disappear from the screen in front of him. There was nothing to prove the exchange had happened, apart from the scrap of paper in his pocket and the buoyancy in his heart. Kanbei closed his laptop and slipped the computer into his backpack. As if on cue, the waiter arrived with a tray of chicken-flavoured rice and soup.

15

Meg hadn't seen the inside of a church in years. Jillian had got married in the botanical gardens and all the memorials for Meg's family had taken place in little chapels at funeral homes. Her parents had scorned God after Helen's accident, but at school Meg had gone to weekly mass like all the other girls. In spite of this she couldn't remember a single word of a single prayer. Mostly she had fantasised about what it might be like to kiss Matthew Adams—the boy who worked at the bakery. She had imagined his hot mouth on hers, unmoved by the pained frown of Jesus above the altar.

Anne's funeral was in a small church with a simple timber cross. There were no thorny crowns or bloodied nails or gold script reminding the parishioners of Jesus' words: *Suffer the little children to come unto me.* It was rustic, even quaint, with its modest altar and matching pair of stained-glass windows. While Jillian parked the car, Meg found an empty pew and peered through the golden haze of dust motes. There were lots of people huddled in groups, shaking their heads and dabbing their eyes with crumpled tissues. She saw Greg at the front looking tired and small in a baggy charcoal suit. Meg felt sorry for him. Helen had once said that the two things people feared most in the world were death and public speaking. If this were true, it seemed particularly vicious to ask the recently bereaved to give a speech to a crowd of friends and family.

Meg remembered Helen's funeral as if it were a dream. She wished someone had spoken to her back then, wished they had explained that the ensuing numbness was not a complete failure of her nervous system, as she had thought, but an important protective mechanism. Rather than being offered platitudes, she wished someone had warned her that for years to come the grief would seize her at inconvenient and unpredictable times, like when she was waiting in line at the supermarket, or eating a sandwich in a park, or reading a newspaper in the library—paroxysms of sorrow that would arrive without warning, like a strike to the head from an unseen stalker. Meg longed to tell Greg all this, but she stayed glued to her seat, paralysed by the ceremony of the proceedings and her own shyness. Instead, she looked down at the 'In Memoriam' card resting in the hammock of her skirt. The photo showed Anne swaddled in a flame-red scarf, her white curls in a wild halo around her face. It struck Meg that even in death Anne was still the brightest thing in the room.

Anne and Helen belonged to a select group of people who left great voids when they departed. For the bereaved—people who'd spent their entire lives in the protective shade of their loved ones—the loss was almost too great to bear. Not just on account of the loneliness, but because of the questions their deaths raised. Who would miss Meg when she died? How many friends, if any, would come to her funeral? She wasn't popular like Anne—she'd be lucky to get a handful of people. And of those people, how many would be really affected by her absence? Not one. Sure, Jillian would have to find someone else to have coffee with, but after a few weeks of polite mourning she'd return to her busy life of pilates and film festivals.

Just then Jillian arrived, red-faced and breathless. She shuffled her way along the pew, apologising as she bumped into people's knees and handbags.

'Parking around here is a nightmare,' she whispered as she sat down beside Meg. She pulled a packet of tissues from her handbag and blotted her sweaty face.

The pastor, a woman, approached the lectern. She was dressed like Anne in a pink shaggy knit—an outfit, perhaps, from Anne's boutique. She began by thanking them all for coming. She explained that the great turnout was a reflection of how loved Anne—who she called Annie—was. She smiled a wide smile and said today would not be a sad day but a celebration of Annie's life. At the word *celebration*, Jillian dug her fingernails into Meg's forearm. Meg looked up, but Jill stared straight ahead at the crown of native flowers on the coffin.

•

Meg was hoping they could avoid tea and cake, but Jillian insisted. 'We really should, for the family,' she said, dragging Meg along by the arm. As they entered the room, Jillian was immediately swept up by the crowd, leaving Meg alone by the hot-water urn. Feeling conspicuous, Meg picked up a lamington and cradled it in her palm. She took a bite of the cake while she watched her friend work the floor. Every so often Jillian would disappear into an embrace only to re-emerge, seconds later, with a hopeful expression.

'And how do you know Anne?'

Meg turned around. The man who had spoken was about her age, with a short clipped beard and a smattering of liver spots around his eyes. He was brightly dressed—some might say inappropriately, given the occasion—in a green tweed jacket and a leather cap.

'I went to school with Anne,' Meg said. 'A long time ago.'

He chuckled, and Meg thought he seemed like the type of man her father would have approved of. 'When you're in your seventies, everything feels like it happened a long time ago,' he said.

Meg returned his smile.

'Actually, that's not completely true,' he went on. 'There are also deaths of friends,' he gestured towards the funeral-goers, 'and births of grandchildren. But those are things you aren't really a part of. Not really.'

Meg finished her lamington, wiped the coconut from her lips. 'And what about you?' she said. 'How do you know Anne?'

The man looked Meg in the eye. 'Anne and I were lovers. A long time ago.'

Meg felt her cheeks burn. She searched the room for Jillian, but her friend was nowhere to be found. The only person she recognised was Greg, and he was crying into a serviette—she could see a smear of raspberry jam on his nose.

'I'm pulling your leg,' the man said, and laughed. 'Annie was a dear friend but nothing more. She liked shy types.'

Meg, who hadn't cried during the funeral, now felt tears prick at the corner of her eyes.

'I'm Patrick,' the man said, and stuck out his hand. Meg put her scrunched-up serviette on the edge of the table and took his hand in hers. His palm was warm and dry.

'Margaret.'

'Ah,' he said, not letting go. 'From the old Persian *margarita*, meaning pearl.'

Meg blushed for the second time in as many minutes.

'It was my mother's name,' he said.

16

On the tram home Andy watched students pore over their lecture notes. Out of habit, he felt for the textbook in his backpack, but didn't pull it out. Normally he would stare at the pages, hoping for something to sink in while he thought of other things, like the way Kiko's lips curled around the end of a pen when she was concentrating. But today, knowing someone else would be sitting his exams for him, Andy was free to daydream, and it was a strange and wonderful thing.

On the walk home from the tram stop, Andy saw things he'd never noticed before. Fallen petals swirling like pink confetti around his feet. A latticework of black branches projected against a teal sky. At this magical hour, even number four Rose Street looked inviting—the amber glow of the windows like pockets of sunshine in the fading light.

When Andy opened the door he was greeted by the smell of melted butter. It reminded him of the Mrs Fields cookie his father had bought him once at the Star Ferry pier in Hong Kong. It was such a rare treat, Andy had savoured every moment—nibbling the edges of the cookie as he watched the boats bob up and down on the harbour.

'Happy birthday!' Mrs Hughes said when she saw him in the doorway to the kitchen. She was wearing an apron over a black blouse, and furry slippers on her feet. In the middle of the kitchen table sat a cake on a wooden chopping board.

Andy checked the date on his phone. Mrs Hughes was right—it was his birthday. He'd forgotten all about it after his parents' generous gift a few days ago. Andy's eyes returned to the cake, which was brown and sticky and crowned with rings of pineapple. His mouth flushed with saliva.

'Would you like a piece?' Mrs Hughes asked.

'Yes please,' he said and sat down at the table.

Mrs Hughes took a knife from the drawer and carved out a large triangle. It made a plopping sound as she dropped it onto the plate. She watched Andy with eager eyes as he plunged his fork into the glossy flesh. The taste was exactly what he'd expected from the smell and look of the thing—syrupy and sweet. It was quite possibly the best birthday present he'd ever received.

'We call it pineapple upside-down cake,' Mrs Hughes said, sitting opposite him. 'Because you flip it over before you serve it.'

Andy shovelled another bite into his mouth. Crumbs clung to his chin. 'You don't want any?' he asked.

'I've had enough cake today,' Mrs Hughes said.

'Pat-a-cake, pat-a-cake, baker's man,' Atticus sang from his cage.

Andy laughed.

'Shoosh, you!' Mrs Hughes said, and waved a finger in mock disapproval before turning back to Andy. 'Did you have a good birthday?'

Andy stopped eating to consider whether he had. 'Yes. Thank you. A very good birthday.'

'What did your parents get for you?'

'Money,' Andy replied, and then, sensing the old lady's disappointment, added, 'It's tradition.'

Mrs Hughes collected Andy's empty plate. 'You know, I was thinking, I'd love to have some Chinese food one of these days.'

Andy looked at the remains of the dessert on the kitchen table. He thought back to the animal-like noises he'd heard through her door the night before last. 'Why don't we go to Chinatown for dinner? For my birthday?'

'Tonight? Really?' Mrs Hughes' eyes flared wide. 'Don't you have to study?'

Andy waved his hand in the air as if shooing the notion away. 'It's a special occasion.'

17

Meg studied herself in the mirror on the dresser. Without make-up she looked like a pale, washed-out image of her real self. But today she refused to indulge in self-pity. Only a few hours ago a man had asked for her phone number, and now she was getting ready to have dinner in the city. She began the fifteen-minute process of drawing herself back to life—powdering the liver spots away, pencilling in her eyebrows, thickening her eyelashes with black mascara. When she was done, she leant back in her chair to review her handiwork. *Everybody has a mirror face*, Helen used to say. Meg's was a subtle raise of the eyebrows and a slight pout of the lips. She was not beautiful—she never had been—but, as her father had said when he was still alive, she had a straight nose, and when she smiled her eyes were really quite lovely.

Andy called an Uber. Meg couldn't remember the last time she'd been to the city, let alone Chinatown. She was amazed by how crowded it was, how hot and bright and loud.

The restaurant was called Shark Fin something. Meg had watched a documentary on TV once about sharks being hunted for their fins. For weeks afterwards she'd been haunted by the image of a finless hammerhead sinking to the ocean bed with frantic eyes.

Inside the restaurant, Meg followed Andy between the maze of tables. When she eventually sat down, breathless, she removed her cardigan and hung it on the back of her chair. Their table was beside an aquarium crammed with mud crabs and groupers. Meg stared at the fish, lying on top of one another on the floor of the tank.

'My father's favourite,' Andy said.

'Poor things.'

'They're okay.' He tapped the glass with his finger. 'They're sleeping.'

The groupers didn't move. They looked like Meg's goldfish, Mr Darcy, before he died. She supposed Andy was just repeating what his parents had told him as a child. For a moment she considered challenging him—forcing him to acknowledge the cruel and crowded conditions inside the tank—but she didn't want to ruin the night. When Andy had suggested dinner, she'd been surprised by the delight she'd felt. She was tired of eating alone, at six o'clock every night. She tried to reassure herself that the groupers in the tank wouldn't recognise their friends when they reappeared, buried in julienned ginger and spring onion.

Just then the waiter arrived. He spoke to Andy in short, sharp Cantonese.

'Would you like something to drink?' Andy asked Meg.

'I'll have a glass of red wine.'

Andy spoke to the waiter for a few minutes—much longer than he needed to translate Meg's order. The waiter laughed and Meg wondered if they were talking about her. Perhaps the waiter was asking Andy what he was doing with this wrinkly old white woman. Perhaps Andy was saying he was adopted, or three-quarters Chinese, and she was actually his grandmother. Surely that would be easier than trying to explain the homeshare program. Either way she was shocked by how different Andy seemed when conversing in his native tongue. She'd never seen him so animated, so chatty.

'He's going to create a menu for us,' Andy said when the waiter had left. 'Something traditionally Chinese.'

Meg drummed her fingers on the thick white tablecloth. Her experience of Chinese cuisine amounted to fried rice and lemon chicken.

'Don't worry,' Andy said. 'I'm paying for everything.'

The waiter arrived with the wine. He uncorked the bottle and filled two glasses to the rim.

Meg smiled at Andy and held up her glass. 'How do you say cheers in Chinese?'

'Gon bui.'

'Gon bui,' Meg said and tapped Andy's glass. As she drank,

she spotted bits of cork floating in the wine, but she didn't say anything. She put the glass down and scooped a piece of debris from the surface with her spoon. 'I feel bad you're using your birthday money on this meal,' she said.

'It was a lot of money,' Andy told her, cleaning his hands with the hot towel the waiter had brought to the table. 'This is nothing.'

'Well, your parents are very generous. Please thank them for me.'

'I will.'

Meg took a sip of the wine. She looked at the label on the bottle—it was a pinot noir from New Zealand. She didn't know much about wine, but it tasted okay to her. While she drank, Andy typed on his phone.

'How's the study?' Meg asked after several minutes had passed.

Andy stopped what he was doing and looked up. 'Sorry,' he said and put his phone facedown on the table. 'The study's fine.'

'Silly me,' Meg said and pressed a crease out of the tablecloth with her palm. 'I'm sure study's the last thing you want to talk about on your birthday.'

'I don't mind.' Andy picked up his glass, swirled the wine inside it. 'Did you go to university?'

'Me?' Meg placed a hand on her chest and laughed. 'God, no. My parents always assumed I'd work or get married when I finished school.'

Andy picked up the bottle of wine and topped up Meg's glass. 'What did you do for a job?'

'Lots of things. I worked in a library, and a bookshop. Later on I got a job at Australia Post.' Meg could feel a buzz from the alcohol. 'But I would've loved to have gone to university.'

Andy raised his eyebrows. 'Really?'

'Oh, yes.'

'What would you have studied?'

Meg ran her finger around the base of the wineglass. 'Literature,' she said and couldn't help but smile as she said it. 'No question.'

Just then the waiter arrived with their dishes—a steamed barramundi and a sizzling hotplate of beef and snow peas. Meg stared at the milky eyes of the fish.

'Would you like some?' Andy asked, his spoon poised above a bowl of white rice.

Meg nodded and stabbed a piece of beef with her fork. She watched Andy use his chopsticks to pick an eyeball from the fish and pop it like a boiled lolly into his mouth. Her stomach churned.

'The eyes and cheeks are the best bits,' Andy said. 'You have to try.'

Meg chewed the piece of beef. It was sweet and tender, but she couldn't bring herself to swallow it. She spat it into her napkin and shovelled some rice into her mouth. 'I'm not a big eyeball fan.'

'Australians like to chop things up and shape them into burgers and sausages so they can pretend they're not eating animals,' Andy said, taking a sip of his wine. 'In Hong Kong we go to the market. We choose a live fish from a bucket and a live chicken from a cage.'

Andy was right, of course, but it hadn't always been that way—Meg remembered going to the butcher as a kid and seeing the carcasses hanging from giant hooks out the back.

'The sausages you eat probably have eyeballs and all sorts of balls in them,' Andy said, and chuckled.

They ate in silence then, listening to the chatter of the other diners and the chink of porcelain and glass. Meg ate the beef while Andy devoured the fish. When she looked up again she saw red blotches blooming like peonies on Andy's neck.

'Are you okay?' she asked. 'You're going red.'

Andy touched his face. 'I'm like my dad. He can't tolerate alcohol either. It's a kind of allergy. It's common in Chinese people.'

'I'm sorry to hear that.'

'It's actually a good thing. I spend less money getting drunk.'

Meg giggled. She could feel the eyes of the other patrons on them, but she couldn't care less. After another glass of red wine her appetite returned and she even tried one of the fish cheeks, which was really nothing more than a crescent-shaped piece of especially sweet flesh.

It was Meg who suggested they catch the tram home. She felt bad that Andy had paid for the Uber and spent so much on dinner—she didn't want him to waste any more money.

'But what about your arthritis?' he said, looking at her knees.

'It's not too bad tonight,' Meg said, moved by his thoughtfulness. She wasn't lying—the alcohol had eased her pain. For the first time in a long time, she felt as if she was floating.

It was nine o'clock and the tram was packed. When Meg hobbled up the steps, a pretty woman in a suit got up and offered her a seat. She thanked the woman and sat down. Andy stood beside her, clinging to a hand-strap. A group of Chinese students were chatting and laughing loudly near the door.

Meg didn't hear the commotion at first, but when the tram came to a stop near the State Library, a man's voice boomed from the back.

'Get out of the way, you fucking Asian cunts,' he yelled as he elbowed his way towards the door. The students stood tall and sucked in their tiny bellies to give the man more room. 'We have rules in this country. We don't pick our noses in public, we don't eat dogs and when we're on a tram we fucking let people through!'

When the doors closed again the tram was quiet. The Chinese students stared at their phones with knotted brows. A man in a pink shirt apologised to them in a soft voice as if he was, in some small way, responsible for what had happened. Meg looked at Andy, who was gazing through the window with a stony face. The red blotches had disappeared from his neck. At each stop, witnesses alighted and fresh passengers got on. After three stops people were chatting again as if nothing had happened. Only the Chinese students remained shaken— their heads hanging, their shoulders collapsed, their chests caving inwards. Meg knew that look. She'd worn it for most of her adolescence—the look of someone willing the earth to open up and swallow them.

18

Andy was lying on his bed. He could feel the sizzling beef at the back of his throat. When he closed his eyes, he saw the tram man's snarling face—the dilated pupils, the tobacco-stained teeth, the spittle on his fissured lips.

Andy had heard about people being abused on public transport before, but he'd dismissed the perpetrators as ignorant, or drunk, or both. Now, having experienced it firsthand, he was surprised by how much it affected him. He was less surprised by his fear. He'd long suspected he was a coward—now he knew it to be true. Like everyone, he'd heard about people who, in a flush of adrenaline, had rushed into blazing buildings or lifted cars with their bare hands. But he'd also read about men and women who'd died during acts of heroism. Nobody on the tram had said or done anything—they'd probably read the articles too. When Andy had looked over at Mrs Hughes, she'd averted her gaze, as if she'd been the one shouting slurs.

Just after ten pm, he was roused by his phone. It was his aunt.

'Happy birthday to you, happy birthday to you, happy birthday dear Andy, happy birthday to you,' she sang in a loud voice.

'Thank you, Auntie.'

'What's the matter? You sound depressed. You're only twenty-two, for God's sake—wait until you get to forty!'

'It's nothing. Just something that happened on the tram.'

'Let me guess—some racist idiot.'

'Yeah.'

'Don't worry about it. It's happened to me plenty of times. After twenty years in Australia I've got skin as thick as a rhinoceros! Try putting up with your very own mother-in-law—the grandmother of your children—rolling her eyes at everything you say!'

Andy had never given much thought to how hard it must have been for his aunt, marrying an Australian. He knew his grandparents had been disappointed at the time, but it hadn't occurred to him that her new Australian family might reject her too.

Winnie's voice softened. 'I know it's hard, being in a new place, with new people.'

Andy felt his throat tighten. The wine had made him emotional. He'd forgotten how funny and kind his aunt could be—it was hard to believe she shared blood with his father.

'When will you be coming to Melbourne again?' Andy asked. 'Maybe we can go for yum cha.'

'Yum cha? In Melbourne?' Winnie said, shocked, as if, rather than lunch, Andy had suggested a trip to the moon. 'Andy, you know I'd love to. But with the kids' school pick-ups and drop-offs and Auskick and ballet and grocery shopping, I hardly have time to do a wee. Australia's not like Hong Kong—you can't just get an amah to do everything for you.' She lowered her voice to a whisper. 'The women here work like slaves.'

Andy forced a laugh.

'You think I'm joking, but it's true. That's why they all look ten years older than they are.'

'My friend's mum said it's because of the hole in the ozone layer.'

Now it was Winnie's turn to laugh. 'That too.'

Andy heard the murmur of a male voice, presumably his uncle Craig's.

'Anyway, I've transferred some birthday lai see to your bank account. You should get it first thing Monday morning.'

'Thank you.'

'Now, don't give that racist dickhead another thought.'

'I won't.'

'Focus on your studies.'

The next morning was Saturday. When Andy got out of bed at eleven, he found himself in an empty house. Mrs Hughes must have left in a rush, because her unwashed teacup and plate were still in the sink. Though she was lazy with dusting, she always washed up after breakfast, and Andy wondered if he should be concerned. He thought about texting her, but worried that might be overstepping some line. She was a grown woman, and this was her house—she could come and go as she pleased.

Andy washed his cup and plate and placed them in the rack to dry. When he was finished, he gazed through the window above the sink at the unruly garden. Buds were sprouting like beads of jade along the branches of the trees, but he could hardly make them out through all the grime on the glass. Feeling restless, he picked up the newspaper lying on the kitchen table, separated the pages and scrunched them into loose paper balls. It took him three hours to clean all the windows, but it was gratifying work. Once he was done, he made himself a cup of coffee and sat back down at the kitchen table to appraise his efforts. The branches looked bright and crisp through the newly polished panes. It reminded Andy of the first time he'd put on spectacles—how amazed he'd been to see the black flecks in the concrete footpath and the people in neighbouring apartments. When he'd described it to his father, his dad said that if change happened slowly, people were less likely to notice it. He'd compared it to parents watching their children grow—it was only when going through old photos that they truly appreciated the transformation.

'Hey diddle diddle, the cat and the fiddle,' Atticus squawked from his cage. Andy had forgotten all about the bird. He looked at the floor of the cage, covered in poo, and opened the door.

'How rude!' Atticus said before jumping out.

Andy removed the soiled paper and buried it in the rubbish bin. He spread clean newspaper over the bottom of the cage, folding the corners in to make a rough circle.

'In possum land the nights are fair!' Atticus said from his perch on the back of a chair.

Andy laughed. 'That's old. Say something new.'

'Something new!'

Andy found a bag of birdseed on a shelf above the cage. He filled up Atticus's bowl. 'There you go.'

'There you go,' Atticus said and hopped back inside the cage. He dipped his beak into the food and re-emerged with a large sunflower seed.

'That wasn't so bad,' Andy muttered to himself as he closed the latch. Perhaps his dad was right—little by little, he could get used to anything.

19

Meg was five minutes early. She hadn't wanted to arrive early, but the bus had made good time. It was a sunny spring day, and people were out walking and cycling. Meg pulled at her skirt. She hadn't been sure what to wear—it was years since she'd been to the boathouse in Fairfield. As she waited, she looked around at the children in scuffed sneakers and the parents in stained and shapeless T-shirts. Feeling conspicuous in her pleated skirt and patent-leather heels, she rubbed her toe in the dirt.

She had been getting out of the shower when she heard her mobile phone ring at nine am. She'd assumed it was Jillian or the phone company—the only people who ever called her these days—but she recognised Patrick's voice straight away.

'Remember me?'

'Maybe,' Meg said, her cheeks flushing.

'It's a bit hot for it, but I was wondering if you'd be up for some scones and tea later today?'

'I'd love that.' Meg wasn't lying—she enjoyed a Devonshire tea.

'I promise to have you back before dark.'

Meg watched Patrick stroll down the muddy embankment, hands tucked into his pockets. He was dressed in slacks and a polo shirt—an outfit that said he cared, but not too much. Meg got out a tissue from her handbag and wiped away some of her lipstick.

'You're looking lovely,' he said when he came within speaking distance.

Meg tugged again at her skirt. A button was digging into her flesh. 'I'm a little overdressed,' she said. She'd planned on being coy, but there was something disarming about him.

'In *Mary Poppins*, Dick Van Dyke wore a candy-striped suit to go punting along the Thames,' Patrick said, jumping up and clicking his heels together. 'So perhaps it's me who's underdressed.'

There was no table service at the boathouse. Patrick ordered two Devonshire teas and carried their tray to a corner table of the balcony. They sat opposite each other. Below them a family of four rowed across the lake.

'Best scones I ever had,' Patrick said as he lathered a scone with whipped butter, 'were from the Peninsula Hotel in Hong

Kong. Fluffy things served with rose-petal jam and clotted cream.'

Meg started at the mention of Hong Kong.

'Have you been?' Patrick asked, sensing her interest.

'Only very briefly.' She picked up a knife and helped herself to a knob of butter. 'But I have a student from Hong Kong living with me at the moment.'

Now it was Patrick's turn to be intrigued. 'So I'm not your only male companion.'

Meg didn't like his teasing tone of voice, but she was pleased to hear him refer to himself as her companion.

'It's called homesharing.'

'Some call it marriage,' Patrick said, and laughed.

'A few months ago, a man broke into my house,' Meg explained. She wanted to make him feel bad for what he'd said. 'I feel safer having someone else around.'

'Of course.' Patrick stuffed the rest of the scone into his mouth. Flour coated his lips.

'I'd be interested to hear what you thought of Hong Kong,' Meg said, in a conciliatory tone. 'My guest doesn't talk much.'

Patrick wiped his mouth with a napkin. 'It's a big city. Like New York but with a lot of Chinese people.' He picked up his cup of tea, took a sip. 'Back then it was filthy—people spat in the street and there were rats the size of cats. Pickpockets were everywhere—you had to be careful. A guy in an electronics shop ripped me off, swapping my camera for a cheaper model after I'd paid for it.'

Meg had been hoping for something more romantic, along the lines of rose-petal jam and clotted cream. 'There must have been something you liked about it?' she said.

Patrick thought for a moment. 'I liked how the waiters at the restaurants gave us hot towels to wipe our hands before and after our meals. And the view from Victoria Peak was rather beautiful. It felt different to be up there, in the mist, away from all the hustle and bustle. As if the air was easier to breathe.'

After scones they sat on a bench by the water. A young boy was feeding the ducks. It was warm in the sunshine, and Meg took off her cardigan. 'Do you have grandchildren?' she asked Patrick.

'I have one granddaughter, Daisy. A miracle child. Born two and a half months early.'

'That must have been hard,' Meg said, hating herself for opening this can of worms. It was too early, too depressing, to talk about her complete lack of family.

'It was hard, at the start,' Patrick said. 'But she's a little firecracker. She wasn't going to let anything stop her from coming into this world.'

Fearful of silence and the questions it might prompt, Meg drew Patrick's attention to the boy throwing oats at the ducks.

'I wish I could be like him. Living in the moment. Not thinking about the past or the future.'

Patrick put his hand next to Meg's, which was clutching the edge of the bench. She felt the brush of his skin and relaxed her grip, just a little.

•

In the car on the way home, they fell into an easy silence. When Meg sneaked a look in Patrick's direction, he was smiling.

'You can turn left here,' she said when they reached the end of her street.

Patrick parked in the driveway. He pulled up the handbrake but left the engine running. 'I don't know why I didn't offer to pick you up,' he said. 'I'm afraid I'm a bit out of practice at this stuff.'

'I take the bus all the time,' Meg lied.

'Well, next time I'll give you a lift.'

'Okay.'

'And I'll wear a candy-striped suit.'

Meg laughed, thanked Patrick and got out of the car. As she picked her way, in heels, down the gravel path to the front door, she was conscious of his eyes on her. Once inside, she flicked off her shoes and stumbled to the kitchen to make herself a cup of tea. The room seemed brighter than when she'd left it—the walls whiter, the colours richer, the windows practically gleaming.

20

Andy didn't hear Mrs Hughes arrive. He was lying on a towel in the backyard, sunning his face and listening to music. His chin had broken out in pimples, and Ming had told him that UV light was good for acne. He'd found the one patch of lawn beneath the jacaranda tree that wasn't choked with weeds. Grass was so precious in Hong Kong, it was often cordoned off with rope like a museum exhibit. Sometimes there was even a small sign erected in the middle, warning people that they risked a heavy fine should they sit or walk or run on it, or do anything other than admire it.

Andy opened his eyes to find Mrs Hughes hovering above him, her hair a white aura around her face. He pulled out his earbuds.

'I didn't hear you get back,' he said, sitting up.

'Don't get up,' she said, and knelt beside him. There was a crunching sound, like tyres on gravel.

'Was that your knees?' Andy asked.

'Yes,' Mrs Hughes sighed.

'Maybe you shouldn't be sitting on the ground.'

'It sounds worse than it feels.' She arranged herself on the grass.

'There's a name for that noise in your knees,' Andy said. 'It's called crepitus.'

'I like it,' Mrs Hughes said. 'It sounds like what it describes.'

'Yes,' Andy agreed.

'We have a word for that too—when something sounds like what it describes. It's called onomatopoeia.'

'Ono what?'

'Onomatopoeia.'

Andy tried, unsuccessfully, to pronounce the funny word. 'It sounds like something a kid made up.'

'I know.' Mrs Hughes shifted position, tucking her legs to one side. 'English is a confusing language. All those silent letters. The _k_ in knife, the _w_ in wrong. What's the point of them?'

For a few minutes they sat listening to the birds and pondering the absurdity of the English language. When they heard Atticus shout 'Mary, Mary, quite contrary!' through the kitchen window, they both laughed.

Mrs Hughes looked around the backyard. 'I don't suppose you know anything about gardening?' she asked.

'Only rich people have houses in Hong Kong,' Andy

replied, picking up a twig from the ground and snapping it in two. 'Some people are so poor they live in cages, like animals. Like Atticus.'

Mrs Hughes frowned. 'Tell me something nice about the place you come from.'

Andy gazed up at the sky as if the answers could be found there. 'In the apartment where I lived as a kid, there was a security guard at the front door. He had a dog called Fei Jai, which means fat boy in Cantonese. After school the guard would let me take Fei Jai for walks. When people saw me with him I'd tell them he was my dog. I liked that.' He pulled a yellow dandelion from the ground and tore the petals off one by one. 'And at the end of the street where we live, there's a place that sells soup noodles. It's very famous in Hong Kong. It has pictures on the walls of all the important people who've come to eat at the restaurant. People like Jackie Chan and Chris Patten—the last governor of Hong Kong. My dad and I would watch the queue from the window of our apartment, and when it got shorter, around ten or eleven pm, we would go down and get a bowl of noodles each. The owner would give us extra dumplings because he knew we were neighbours. It's the most delicious soup I've ever had.'

Mrs Hughes massaged her knee. 'My favourite memory is baking pear and rhubarb crumble with my mum. I remember rubbing butter into the biscuit crumbs and the smell—that sweet, warm vanilla smell.'

'The olfactory bulb is the part of the brain responsible for smell. It connects directly to the memory centre,' Andy said.

'Is there anything you don't know?' Mrs Hughes laughed.

Andy thought about the upcoming exam, and his meeting with Kanbei. 'Lots of things.'

The sun had fallen behind the neighbour's wall. Andy shivered.

'Can I ask you something, Andy?' Mrs Hughes said.

'Of course.'

'Do you think it's crazy for a woman my age to start dating again?'

Andy swallowed, his throat dry. Had the old lady misinterpreted his invitation to Chinatown the other night? Was this her way of propositioning him? Panicked, he turned away.

'I'm sorry,' Mrs Hughes said. 'It was a silly question. It's just that I had lunch with a man today...'

On hearing this, Andy felt relieved, and then ashamed.

'His name's Patrick. A widower.'

Andy was genuinely shocked that Mrs Hughes had been on a date. But when he saw her gloomy face and the nervous way she rubbed at a spot on her skirt, he couldn't help but feel a little sorry for her. 'I don't think it's crazy,' he lied.

The old lady studied her hands. Andy stared at them too—at the branching blue tributaries of her veins, at the scaly patches that were probably early skin cancers.

'I do,' she said.

NOVEMBER

21

For a long time Meg sat on the toilet and stared at the blood. It was the middle of the night and she'd got up as she did every night, around one am, to use the toilet. She hadn't had any pain and the blood had come as a shock. It wasn't a lot—just a small blot on the paper—but it had been twenty years since she'd experienced such a thing. She searched the cupboard beneath the sink and was relieved to find a packet of Helen's old incontinence pads behind the first-aid kit.

At her last appointment, the GP had told Meg she wouldn't need pap smears anymore. The doctor hadn't explained why, but Meg understood. If cervical cancer hadn't got her yet, it probably never would—she would most certainly die from something else, like a heart attack, before it could. But the

GP had also warned her that bleeding after menopause was a bad sign, and that if it ever happened, Meg should make an appointment to see her straight away. 'It's a red flag,' the doctor had said, laughing. 'Excuse the pun.'

Meg couldn't sleep. The pad felt bulky, like a nappy between her legs. She stared at the ceiling in the dark, remembering how she'd locked herself in the shed and waited to die the day she got her first period. Her mother had finally coaxed her out to explain that she was not, in fact, haemorrhaging to death as she had concluded, but going through a normal developmental process. Her mum had then launched into a very brief, but nonetheless embarrassing, spiel about how babies were made. Meg remembered feeling betrayed. She'd preferred the idea that a baby was a magical gift, dropped in clean white sheets from the beak of a stork onto a freshly swept doorstep, instead of something born of blood and cramps and incapacitating mood swings. It was the last and most alarming of a string of disappointing confessions—that it was her mother, rather than the tooth fairy, who'd sneaked into her bedroom to bury a coin beneath her pillow; that it was her father, rather than Santa Claus, who for years had eaten the biscuit and drunk the port on Christmas Eve. If life had turned out differently and she'd had children of her own, Meg wasn't sure she'd have been able to tell them such fibs.

She closed her eyes, and Patrick's smiling face appeared behind her lids. She wondered what a man like him wanted with an old woman like her. She was not worldly or funny or wise. She was not rich or smart or beautiful. While flattered by his attention, she was also suspicious of it. Last month she'd watched a current affairs program about a widow who'd given her life savings to a con man from Nigeria. But Patrick drove an expensive car and dined at fancy restaurants—Meg was quite sure he wasn't after her money.

She'd only ever had sex with two men—Terry Costas, the bookish Greek boy who'd lived across the road when she was growing up, and Tim O'Malley, her boss at the post office. The sex with Terry was terrible—being virgins, neither of them had any idea what they were doing. Terry had got a cramp in his calf muscle the first time, and the second time Meg's earring had got tangled in his hair. But Meg had loved Terry for his patience, and the gentle way he'd traced a figure eight across her back with his fingertips after the sex was over. They'd only done it a handful of times before Meg had ended it for fear of being discovered by her father. It was the 1960s and the beginning of the sexual revolution, but sex before marriage was still a scandalous thing in suburban Melbourne. Terry had travelled to Greece soon after Meg had called things off—sometimes, in a moment of self-indulgence, she wondered if she'd broken his heart. Months later, his parents—who knew nothing—had told her he'd died in a motorbike accident in Athens. Meg had offered her polite condolences before running home to bawl into her pillow.

Tim, a married man, had arrived in Meg's life decades later, when she was well into her forties and had resigned herself to a life without marriage and children. She didn't love Tim, but he was a kind and generous lover. He rarely spoke of his family and it was easy for Meg to pretend he was single— not because she was jealous, but because she didn't like to think of someone being hurt by what they were doing. The sex with Tim was better than with Terry, if a little stressful— moments stolen in the back room amid the packages, at the end of Meg's shift. Tim couldn't get home too late or his wife would become suspicious. But the speed and efficiency had suited Meg too—she was busy caring for her dying mother and looking after Helen. When they'd ended the affair, it was with the same businesslike amicability with which they'd conducted their relationship—neither of them had shed a tear. There had been nobody since.

Lying in bed, Meg calculated that it had been thirty years since anyone other than Helen had seen her naked. Once, long ago, she'd had a figure she was proud of. She wasn't tall and slim like Helen, but she had a nice womanly silhouette. Now grey hairs sprouted from her chin and nipples, and her skin hung slack, like old trackie dacks, from her bones. She couldn't imagine anyone, let alone someone as elegant as Patrick, wanting to get anywhere near her.

Meg wondered if old men stayed up late too, thinking about such things. It seemed to her that age was kinder to them. Men had drugs to help them have sex. If they wanted to, they could father children well into their eighties. Women's fertility ended at menopause, after which they grew shapeless and hairy. Meg recalled her mother's shrivelled body on her deathbed, her once-lovely breasts sad and shrunken.

Perhaps, Meg pondered, instead of a disease, the return of her period signalled a restoration of her fertility—a miraculous reversal of the ageing process. Maybe tomorrow she would wake up with a smooth face and a flat belly. She thought of

Andy and tried to remember how she'd felt at twenty-two. In hindsight, she wished she'd been having sex with boys and touring the world with Anne and Jillian, instead of baking cakes with her mum and reading books at the library. But it was easy to think that now, after the fact. Terry and Tim had pursued her. If they hadn't, Meg knew nothing would have happened. And while she'd enjoyed the sex, she'd felt guilty— with Terry because she was young and unmarried, and with Tim because of his wife and family.

Meg was born shy. According to her parents, as a little girl she'd spent entire family gatherings hiding behind her mother's skirt. Things had only got worse when she'd turned five—the year she'd started school, and Helen had arrived. Her sister was a difficult baby from the start, loud and sleepless and constantly demanding attention. One time, on Boxing Day, when Meg was seven and Helen was two, her parents had got halfway to Dromana before they realised they'd left Meg at home. That day, like most days, she'd been swinging on the hanging tyre in the backyard, her head buried in a book. Even then, Meg had preferred to be on her own. People bored her with their dumb questions. She would much rather be reading about the adventures of Alice in Wonderland and Anne of Green Gables, or writing her own stories about smart, feisty girls who forced the world to take notice of them. But those had been the golden years before the fear, before Helen's terrible accident.

22

Andy found Ming in the library. Unlike the other students, slumped in their seats with unwashed hair and bloodshot eyes, Ming was sitting erect, with a straight, taut spine. On the desk beside his laptop, three sharp pencils were arranged in neat parallel lines.

Andy pulled out one of Ming's earplugs.

Ming snapped his laptop shut. 'Why don't you say hello like a normal person?' he said. 'With a tap on the shoulder or something?'

'You've known me for two years now,' Andy said, taking a seat beside his friend. 'You should know I'm not normal.'

A girl at an adjacent desk glared at them.

'Let's get a coffee,' Andy whispered.

'I can't,' Ming said, opening his laptop again. On the screen were the multiple-choice questions from the past exam paper that had been doing the rounds. 'The microbiology exam's next week.'

'You know,' Andy said, waving his finger, 'studies have shown that caffeine improves concentration.'

'I'll have a coffee on the morning of the exam, then.' Ming put his earplug back in.

Andy had known it was a long shot—when it came to swot vac, Ming didn't socialise—but he desperately wanted some company. He left the library and roamed the campus. It was November and the sun was warm. A couple of students were kicking a footy to each other across the lawn. Otherwise the place was deserted. Andy supposed most people were at home or in the library, cramming for the upcoming exams. The few who were lounging on the grass looked defeated—staring into space with vacant eyes.

He walked towards the coffee shop. When he'd first arrived in Melbourne he'd been baffled by Australians' love of bitter drinks. He'd never been able to stomach beer—it made him sleepy and itchy—but he'd started drinking coffee after reading about the effect of caffeine on academic performance. As a chronic insomniac, he was quickly hooked.

Today he ordered a flat white. While he waited, he looked out through the window at the courtyard. He recognised Kiko straight away. She was sitting at one of the outside tables, bent over a textbook, sipping her drink, which Andy knew must be a hot chocolate. Whenever he followed Kiko to the café after lectures, she always ordered a hot chocolate.

As he watched her, his heart fluttered. He remembered his conversation with Mrs Hughes a few weeks ago. Surely if a woman her age could find the courage to put herself out there, Andy could too: When his coffee was ready, he picked it up and opened the glass door.

Kiko sensed his presence in the courtyard immediately. She looked up from her textbook and smiled.

'Is anybody sitting here?' Andy said with a croaky voice.

'No,' Kiko said and gestured to an empty chair.

Andy sat down. He cleared his throat—he'd had a cold recently and couldn't seem to shake it.

'Are you okay?' Kiko asked, and offered him her water bottle.

Andy nodded. He took a sip of her water. It was not lost on him that his mouth was on the same spot that Kiko's lips had been just minutes before.

'Aren't we in a few lectures and pracs together?' she asked.

'Yeah, I think so.' While Andy was thrilled that Kiko had recognised him, he was disappointed she wasn't sure where she knew him from. 'Microbiology.'

Kiko closed her laptop. 'You ready for the exam?'

Andy thought of Kanbei in his black hoodie. 'As ready as I'll ever be.'

Kiko's face dropped. 'Gram-negative, gram-positive. It's all so confusing.'

Andy stuck out his hand. 'I'm Andy.'

She surrendered three slim fingers to Andy's palm. 'Kiko Mathews.'

Andy pretended he hadn't practised writing her name over

and over in the margins of his notebook. 'Is that Japanese?'

'Yes, my mother's Japanese.'

It was not unusual to see Eurasians in Hong Kong. They stood out with their brown hair and round, double-lidded eyes.

'Do you go back much?' he asked.

'Every two years, to see my cousins.'

He'd always wanted to visit Japan. He pictured cherry blossoms, fast trains and quaint houses with paper walls.

'Do you speak Japanese?' he asked.

'Hai.'

Andy recognised the word for *yes*. It was very similar to Cantonese.

'And what about you?' Kiko asked.

'The only thing I know is that you say moshi moshi to answer the phone.'

'No.' Kiko laughed. 'I mean where are you from?'

'Oh.' Andy studied the dried milk on the plastic lid of his coffee. 'Hong Kong.'

'I love Hong Kong!'

Surprised, Andy looked up.

'I love the lights and the food and the Star Ferry,' Kiko said.

Andy rarely crossed the harbour on the Star Ferry—it was quicker to take the train. But talk of home stirred something inside him. He thought of his mother, roaming the psychiatric ward in her pyjamas, and his father, eating instant noodles alone in the kitchen.

Kiko must have seen the change in his face. 'Is something wrong?'

Andy shook his head. 'No, I'm just hungry. Do you want to get some lunch? I know a place that does good pho just off campus.'

She glanced at the time on her phone. 'I really should be studying. I need to brush up on my gram stains.'

Andy thought of Mrs Hughes again. 'How about after the exam?'

Kiko considered this. 'I guess I'll need a break before neuroscience,' she said.

Andy told her his number, and Kiko punched it into her phone. Her fingers were long and slender, her nails perfect pink discs.

'I'll send you a missed call,' she said.

Despite the warning, Andy jumped when his phone vibrated in his pocket. His sweat glands were pumping like sprinklers; his heart was pounding against his breastbone. As they said their goodbyes, Andy felt both relieved to be rid of Kiko and desperate to see her again.

23

Meg prepared the table. She'd never invited a man to her house for dinner before. Earlier that day, Patrick had said he'd like to see where she lived, and Meg, drunk with flattery, had said he should pay a visit. But instead of nominating a date later in the week, which would have given her some time to go to the shops and buy ingredients for dinner, she'd agreed to his suggestion of that night.

Meg was relieved to hear Andy's key in the lock at five o'clock. It would be good to have a chaperone, someone to ensure Patrick didn't try anything. As much as Meg would love to know what that might feel like after all these years, she did worry about her sagging breasts and ill-fitting dentures. She didn't expect Andy to refuse to stay.

'I don't want to get in the way,' he explained.

'You won't,' Meg said. 'Please?'

Andy shook his head.

'But you have to eat.'

'I'll eat something quick in my room. I have an exam next week.'

Meg was starting to think Andy didn't like her cooking. She decided to try a different tack. 'This can be your ten hours of mandatory service.'

That got Andy's attention. He looked up at her with defeated eyes. Meg felt bad then, but not so bad as to let him off the hook.

'It won't take ten hours. One and a half, maybe two.'

Meg picked flowers from the garden while Andy showered and dressed. She'd just finished arranging the kangaroo paws in a vase when the doorbell rang. She looked at the clock on the wall—Patrick was ten minutes early. When Meg checked herself in the mirror in the hallway, her reflection seemed especially pale. Maybe it was just nerves, or maybe she'd lost more blood than she thought.

'One minute!' she called through the door before rushing to the bedroom to apply some blush. When she re-emerged she was amazed to find Andy and Patrick chatting and laughing in the hall.

'The door was open,' Patrick said. 'And then I bumped into Andy.'

'Patrick speaks Cantonese!' Andy exclaimed.

'Not really,' Patrick said, taking off his hat. 'I can say, *how are you, where's the toilet* and some other things I'd rather not repeat in front of Margaret.'

Andy laughed in his boyish way, half snort, half chuckle.

Meg was delighted to see the two of them getting along—she'd been feeling guilty about pressuring Andy into the role of chaperone. 'Come in,' she said and led them past the lounge towards the kitchen.

Meg had considered setting up the dining room, but every meal she'd eaten there, enveloped by the floral wallpaper and heavy curtains, had felt suffocating. Looking at the kitchen table now, with its plastic tablecloth and droopy kangaroo paws, Meg wondered if she'd made the wrong decision. She uncorked the bottle of red wine Patrick had brought with him and filled three large wineglasses. She hoped the more they had to drink, the less the plastic tablecloth and limp flowers would bother them.

While Meg finished preparing the pasta sauce, Patrick spoke of his time in Hong Kong. As it turned out, the hotel he'd stayed in all those years ago wasn't far from the apartment where Andy's parents lived now. Patrick impressed Meg with his new-found enthusiasm for the city. She assumed he was indulging Andy, and therefore her, and for this she was thankful. She topped up his glass of red wine before turning her attention back to the stove. Her guests chatted happily, only stopping when she emptied the kettle into the saucepan with a mighty hiss.

'Hot potato, hot potato!' Atticus screeched.

Patrick turned to the cage behind him, which was partly hidden by the kitchen door. 'You didn't tell me you had an African grey!' he said, clearly thrilled.

Meg snapped a bundle of spaghetti in half and dropped it into the pot. She wiped her hands on her apron before walking around the kitchen table to open the cage.

'Waltzing Matilda, waltzing Matilda, you'll come a-waltzing Matilda with me,' Atticus sang, strutting towards Meg and clambering onto her outstretched hand.

'Would you like to hold him?' she asked, extending her arm to Patrick.

'Yes please,' Patrick said. Atticus shuffled from Meg's hand onto the cuff of his sleeve and paused, lifting his feet up and down as if he'd stepped in something sticky.

'My brother had an African grey parrot,' Patrick said, slowly raising his arm to look Atticus in the face. The bird tilted his head, mirroring Patrick's quizzical expression.

Meg returned to the stove to stir the pasta, separating the strands of spaghetti with her fork. So, Patrick was a bird person, like her. There was still so much she didn't know about this man, and she felt excited at the prospect of more surprises, other things they might have in common.

Andy coughed. Lately he'd been coughing a lot. Meg wondered if she should prompt him to see a doctor. Was that part of her duty of care as his host? Maybe they could go to the clinic together—he for his cough and she for her bleeding. She would suggest it tomorrow. For now they would enjoy their dinner. She plated up her signature spaghetti bolognese and gave it a light sprinkle of parmesan cheese.

'Fine and dandy!' Atticus squawked before flapping up into the air and onto Patrick's head. He pulled at a few strands of hair with his beak before hopping down onto Patrick's shoulder.

Meg wiped her hands on a tea towel. 'C'mon, you,' she said, scooping Atticus up. She could tell Andy found the presence of animals at mealtimes distasteful. When the bird was safely locked away, Meg dispensed the plates and topped up the wineglasses. She urged Patrick and Andy to sit down.

Andy was the first to notice the stain on Patrick's collar. He pointed at it, speechless, with a look of horror. Unfazed, Patrick dabbed the spot with his serviette. 'My brother's bird used to vomit on me all the time. Apparently it's a sign of affection.'

Meg watched, overjoyed, as Patrick used the bread to soak up the last of the pasta sauce. As usual, Andy had only played with his meal—flattening and spreading it across the plate to give the impression he had eaten it. But Meg would not be disheartened. They'd spoken of many things tonight—birds and travel and books and movies—and Andy had only looked bored once or twice.

It was nine o'clock. Ordinarily Meg would be in bed by now, but tonight she busied herself making an impromptu dessert of tinned peaches, vanilla ice-cream and fresh mint from the garden.

'I suppose you'd be too young to remember life before the handover?' Patrick asked Andy as Meg got the ice-cream from the freezer.

'I was just a baby,' Andy said, somewhat hesitantly.

Meg recalled seeing something on the news years ago,

with Helen, about Britain returning Hong Kong to China.

'You have to give credit to the British,' Patrick said. 'They don't just jump ship like the French. They always leave good government behind.'

Meg watched Andy bury a mint leaf in his ice-cream.

'Hong Kong, Singapore, India—they've all done pretty well for themselves,' Patrick went on, wiping his mouth with his serviette. 'And that's in large part because of the British.'

Andy took a bite of slippery peach as Patrick reeled off a list of failed French colonies.

'Did I mention that Andy's studying biomedicine?' Meg interrupted.

'Yes, I think you told me the other day.' Patrick leant back in his chair, and Meg marvelled at how youthful his movements were—it was hard to believe he was in his seventies. 'I did biology at university, you know,' he added.

Andy looked up and made eye contact with Patrick then, which Meg took to be a good sign.

'Back then we studied for the love of it. To satisfy a genuine scientific curiosity.' Patrick nudged Andy's elbow. 'When we weren't chasing the ladies.'

Andy forced a smile.

'Now students see science as a stepping stone to medicine— they want to be neurosurgeons and make lots of money.'

Meg didn't know if Andy wanted to be a doctor—they'd never discussed such details—but she saw him bristle at Patrick's words. 'It's getting late,' she said, standing up. She felt all the pain of the night's activities flood her knees.

'Let me clean up,' Patrick offered.

'Yes, I'll help you,' Andy said, pushing back his chair.

Meg shook her head. 'I think it's best if we call it a night. Andy can give me a hand with the dishes in the morning.'

Andy agreed and dropped his plate in the sink. Meg said she'd walk Patrick to his car.

Outside, the moon was just a sliver, and the smell of jasmine hung thick in the air. 'I had fun tonight,' Patrick said when they reached his car. He leant his head towards Meg and slid his hot fingers across the back of her neck. She gasped. Perhaps Patrick heard this, or perhaps he felt the tension in her muscles and the hammer of her pulse beneath her skin. Either way, he stopped what he was doing. Meg felt the tug of tiny strands of hair as he pulled his hand away.

24

Andy collapsed onto his bed. Springs groaned in protest. He looked at his phone on the bedside table, picked it up and typed a message to Kiko. He pressed send before he could change his mind.

Hi.

For all he knew, Kiko could be sleeping, or her phone could be turned off. He held his breath.

Hi.

His fingers trembled as he typed.

How's the study going?

Crap.

Me too.

How come?

I rent a room from an old lady. Tonight I had dinner with her and her boyfriend.

The old lady has a boyfriend?

Andy laughed. *Yes.*

What's he like?

Old. A racist.

A pause. Pulsing dots. *Really?*

He spent most of dinner telling me I should be grateful to the British.

For what?

For making Hong Kong a success.

OMG. That's awful.

Andy imagined Kiko at home. For some reason he assumed she still lived with her parents. He pictured her sitting on her childhood bed, in her pyjamas, her black hair long and loose. He was about to type a reply when he was interrupted by a knock at the door. It was a quiet knock—so quiet he thought he'd imagined it—until he heard the whisper that followed.

'Andy? Are you still awake?'

For a moment he considered pretending to be asleep, but there was something in Mrs Hughes' voice—an anxiety he couldn't ignore. What if she and Patrick had argued? What if she was feeling unwell? Was there something in his contract about duty of care? Andy plugged his phone into its charger and opened the door.

Mrs Hughes hesitated as she entered the room. She looked at his Ikea bedspread and the sketches of Kiko taped to the wall.

'Please, sit down,' Andy said.

'Thank you.' She perched on the very edge of the chair beside the desk, as if not wanting to take up too much space. Andy sat on the bed, facing her.

'I wanted to apologise,' she began, massaging her knee, 'for Patrick.'

Andy had been primed for something serious—a medical emergency, a fight, a break-up. He regretted ending his conversation with Kiko to open the door.

'I was worried he'd offended you,' Mrs Hughes said. She stopped massaging her knee and wrung her hands. 'With what he'd said. Not like the man on the tram the other day, not that bad, but all the same...'

Andy shook his head. 'It's not your fault.'

Mrs Hughes stared at the frayed rug on the floor. Andy gazed out at the starry sky.

'Was this your daughter's room?' he said, after several seconds had passed.

Mrs Hughes looked up, her trance broken. 'I don't have a daughter. This was my sister's bedroom. She died a few years ago.'

Andy's heart sank. He'd been hoping to guide the conversation to happier subjects. 'I'm sorry.'

To his surprise, the old lady laughed. 'It's not your fault.'

They didn't speak often, but it struck Andy that on the rare occasions they did, he and Mrs Hughes spent a lot of time apologising to each other.

'She had an accident when she was young,' Mrs Hughes said. 'You may have noticed the ramp in the front and back yards, the rails in the bathroom.'

Andy nodded. He had noticed, but he'd assumed they were recent additions, for Mrs Hughes.

'We were in the backyard one afternoon. She was eleven and I was sixteen. I was ignoring her, reading a book, and she was doing tricks in the tree to get my attention. Helen never stood still, never stopped, always climbing and running and dancing. I was the opposite—too shy and fearful to do anything. Anyway, that day Helen was doing acrobatics in the tree. She kept taunting me, *Bet you can't do this*, but I was ignoring her. I was deep in my book—a gothic novel called *Rebecca*. I remember the exact line I was reading when I heard her scream. *We're not meant for happiness, you and I.* When I looked up, Helen was lying on the ground, howling, with her legs at unnatural angles.'

'Spinal cord injury?'

'Yes. I remember I put the book down on the grass, open at that page. As if, even as my sister cried, I didn't want to lose my place in the story. The book lay there for weeks afterwards, getting ruined. It got soaked in the rain and then dry and crinkly in the sun, but I didn't touch it. I guess someone, Mum probably, must have picked it up eventually. But I never finished it. I couldn't bear to. I never found out what happened.'

'How bad were your sister's injuries?'

'She fractured a couple of vertebrae in her back, which left her with no feeling in her legs at all. She never walked again after that.'

For a minute Mrs Hughes stared into space, remembering something. Andy snatched a look at his phone. There were no new messages from Kiko. He guessed she was waiting for him to reply. When he looked up again, the old lady's eyes were shiny with tears.

'I'm boring you,' she said.

'No, not at all.'

She pulled a tissue from a box on the desk and dabbed the corners of her eyes. 'Do you have brothers or sisters?'

Andy placed his phone facedown on the bed. 'My mother got sick after I was born. The doctor said she shouldn't have any more children.' It was the first time he had talked about his mother's illness with anyone.

'It's common. My friend Jill had dreadful problems with her blood pressure when she was pregnant.'

Andy shook his head. 'It was psychological. Postnatal depression.' Nobody had ever told Andy this, but he'd figured it out for himself.

'So you've missed out on things too. Life can be lonely for an only child.'

In Andy's mind, it was his parents who'd made all the sacrifices. His mother had forfeited her health to give his father a son. His father had spent every waking hour making money to put Andy through private school and university. His parents reminded him of this on a regular, if not daily, basis. But Mrs Hughes' words resonated with him. He'd grown up alone, no brothers or sisters for company. And his parents were often busy, too preoccupied to play with him. At worst he felt like a burden; at best, a nuisance. On arriving in Melbourne he was shocked to see how affectionate Australian families were in public. Sometimes on the tram he liked to watch

120

parents with their children. He saw mothers press their lips to their toddlers' heads and inhale, as if sitting beside them wasn't enough—they needed to breathe them in.

'Sometimes I fantasise about being a mother,' Mrs Hughes said. 'But I know it can take quite a toll.'

Thinking of his mother made Andy's throat feel tight and dry. He was glad when Mrs Hughes kept talking.

'I never got married, because I was too busy caring for others—firstly, for my sick mother, and later, for Helen.' She studied her slippers on the floor.

Andy thought of his parents. 'I don't think I'll get married.'

'It would be nice to have some company,' Mrs Hughes said. Her eyes flicked up to the sketches of Kiko on the wall. Andy looked away, embarrassed. He picked up his phone. Before he could check his messages again he heard what sounded like the crack of a twig outside the window. Mrs Hughes had gone pale. She pointed to the light switch. Andy remembered that the woman at the agency had said something about a break-in. He turned off the light and peered through the curtains. Mrs Hughes hovered behind him. When his eyes had adjusted to the dark, he made out the crouched figure of a man near the fence, just a few metres from the window. Mrs Hughes gasped—she'd seen the man too. Together they watched him scale the fence into the next-door neighbour's backyard. They heard another snap of twigs as his body hit the ground on the other side.

'We have to call the police,' Andy whispered, letting go of the curtain.

Mrs Hughes' breathing was fast and shallow. 'That's

Judith's place. She's deaf. She won't hear a thing, until it's too late.'

Andy picked up his phone. There was a message from Kiko, but he didn't read it. Instead, he called 000 and asked for the police. The operator transferred him to another woman who asked a slew of questions—many of them relevant but many of them not. Mrs Hughes sat down again in the chair by the desk. She closed her eyes, but her frown remained. Andy was on the phone for nearly ten minutes. When he hung up, he touched her gently on the shoulder.

'You should go to bed,' he said.

'The police will want to talk to us when they get here.'

As if on cue, they heard a knock at the front door.

'I'll speak to them,' Andy said. He'd never been interviewed by a police officer before. His heart was doing somersaults in his chest, but his voice was steady.

'That's good of you, Andy, but I should probably speak to them too—they might want to know about the other break-in.'

They walked down the hallway together. Before opening the door, Mrs Hughes stopped and turned to face him. 'I've been meaning to ask you—have you been cleaning the windows?' It wasn't clear from the look on her face whether she was happy about this or not.

'Yes—I hope that's okay.'

She didn't respond straight away. It was only after another impatient rap at the door that she placed her hand on Andy's arm.

'Thank you.'

25

When Jillian called to suggest coffee the next day, Meg was bursting to talk. Ever since Anne's funeral, her friend had seemed a little flat. Meg was excited to have some news to share with her. At Café Bonjour she told Jillian about Patrick and the boathouse and how he'd leant in to kiss her when she'd walked him to his car. She told her about eating Chinese food in the city with Andy, and the man on the tram who'd shouted at the students. She told her about calling the police on the trespasser, and how Andy had taken control of the situation. As she spoke, she suppressed her delight at the stunned look on Jillian's face.

'Two intruders in six months?' Jillian said, licking the froth from her skinny decaf latte. 'You've got to move out of that place.'

'You didn't let me finish,' Meg said. 'The intruder was actually Bev's grandson.' She lowered her voice. 'He was drunk. The police said he wet himself when they shone their torch at him.'

Bev was the grumpy widow who lived three doors down from Meg. Everybody had a tale about Bev and her good-for-nothing grandson. But Jillian wasn't interested in Bev and her problems. She put her cup down and clasped her hands together on the table.

'Forget those two. What I want to know is what you're going to do about Patrick.'

Meg sighed. She should have known this was the part of the story that would most intrigue Jillian. 'I'm going to call it off.'

Jillian raised her eyebrows. 'Why?'

Meg thought of Patrick's boorish behaviour the night before. 'We don't have that much in common.'

'You're both alive, aren't you?'

'I just don't see the point of it all,' Meg said.

'What's the point of anything we do?' Jillian sat back in her chair. 'At our age, other than eating and sleeping, everything's pointless.' She dropped her voice to a whisper. 'Even sex.'

Meg blushed. Her friend was right.

'You know, I used to feel sorry for you,' Jillian said, her tone biting. 'You gave up so much to care for your mother, and for Helen—I thought it was admirable. But now I think you were just scared. Scared of making a life for yourself.'

Meg bristled. When things got tough, Jillian had always paid others to do the hard work for her—a nanny for the kids, a night nurse for her dying mother. Meg didn't have that luxury.

When the waitress arrived with the bill, instead of throwing five dollars onto the table like she normally did, Meg let Jillian pay. Outside, she followed Jillian to her red Mazda, which was parked near the corner in front of the pilates studio. They rode in silence in the car.

'How's the Chinese boy going?' Jillian asked when they stopped at an intersection. Meg knew this was her friend's way of apologising—softening her voice, feigning interest.

'His name's Andy,' Meg said. 'And it was good to have him around the other night.'

'For the intruder who wasn't an intruder.'

Meg thought of responding with some smart remark about a friend who wasn't a friend, but then thought better of it. She stared out the window at the powerlines sagging overhead.

Andy wasn't home when Meg got back. She filled and boiled the kettle and opened the door to Atticus's cage.

'Pat-a-cake, pat-a-cake, baker's man,' Atticus sang as he climbed onto her hand. Meg scratched the smoke-coloured feathers around his neck. She took him outside into the backyard and sat down on the stone bench beneath the jacaranda.

Meg's mother had always kept the backyard pretty before she became too frail to tend to it. For years after her death, Meg had paid a local handyman to weed and prune the garden, but when he'd fallen off a roof and broken his leg she hadn't looked for a replacement. That was six months ago. Now the garden was thick and wild. The house on Rose Street was the only home Meg had ever known, and she couldn't even take care of it. Perhaps Jillian was right. Perhaps she'd been a coward, hiding from the world, using Helen and her mother as an excuse. Perhaps if she'd gone to university and got herself a well-paying job like Jillian, she could've employed a nurse and had her own family. Perhaps if she'd done that she wouldn't be alone now, using cheap rent to lure a young man to stay with her, for companionship and the illusion of security.

Meg was still going over all this in her mind when she heard the phone ring inside the house. By the time she got to it she was breathless.

'Hello?' she croaked into the receiver.

'Margaret?'

It was Patrick. He insisted on calling her Margaret even though she'd told him many times to call her Meg. All his life he'd been Pat or Paddy or Patto, he said—only his mother had called him Patrick. He was ringing to invite Meg to join him for a few days away on the coast.

Meg stared at the fridge door. Her eyes flicked from the magnet Jillian had brought back as a souvenir from Paris to the mugshot-style photo of the Bangladeshi boy she sponsored through World Vision.

'Well?' Patrick said after several seconds had passed.

'Yes.'

Now it was Patrick's turn to pause. 'Yes?' he repeated, as if he couldn't believe it.

'Yes,' Meg said again.

26

Ming waved his hand in front of Andy's face. 'Man, you're like a zombie today!'

They were in the one section of the library where chatting was permitted. A few noisy groups of students were working on projects around them. Normally Ming would be holed up in his apartment until the very last hour before the exam, but he'd texted Andy that morning, inviting him to catch up for lunch.

Andy told his friend what had happened the night before. How the police had arrived at midnight, and how, after speaking to them, he hadn't been able to sleep.

'Hasn't this place been broken into before?' Ming said. 'Where do you live now? The ghetto?'

Andy explained that this time the burglar was actually just a drunk teenager, lost on his way home.

Ming shook his head. 'I don't understand why people drink alcohol. Why would you want to feel out of control?'

Andy sneaked a look at Ming's hands. The eczema had made his knuckles dry and scaly, like the skin of a lizard.

'Are you hungry?' Ming asked.

Andy nodded.

'Let's get some sushi.'

They crossed the campus in silence. Andy sensed something was up. In the food court, they ordered and paid for their sushi and walked to an empty table in the courtyard. Finally, when Andy was biting into his tempura roll, Ming revealed what was on his mind.

'This is what my dad's getting me if I get straight H1s on my exams,' he said, putting his iPhone on the table. On the screen was a picture of a car—a glossy, black, expensive-looking car. Andy didn't know what make it was—he'd never been interested in such things. But Ming seemed unperturbed by his lack of enthusiasm. He pushed the phone even further towards Andy. 'It's the latest SLC Mercedes.'

Andy wiped the soy sauce from his lips. 'That's great.'

'I'll take you for a spin during the break, when I get back from Hong Kong. We can drive down to Brighton.'

Andy knew Ming would get straight H1s. Ming always got straight H1s. And Ming's father always bought him an outrageous reward. Andy couldn't help but think of his own father, shuttling back and forth between home and the hospital, the two lines between his eyes growing deeper with each passing day.

'I've got a date with Kiko,' he said, without thinking.

Ming put the phone back in his pocket. 'I don't believe you.'

For all Ming's talk about sex and women, Andy had always suspected he'd had little experience with them.

'After the micro exam. We're going for pho.'

Ming scoffed. 'That doesn't count!'

'Two people having a meal, alone.'

Ming stirred a large dollop of wasabi into his pool of soy sauce. Andy felt satisfied that he had, at the very least, taken some of the shine off his friend's fancy car. Neither of them spoke as they finished their sushi.

Ming closed his empty sushi box and wrapped the rubber band around it. Only minutes ago he'd been buzzing with excitement, but now he looked dull and deflated. 'I'd better get back to the library,' he said.

As Andy walked to the tram, he was overwhelmed by regret. Not just because he'd upset Ming, but because in talking up his meeting with Kiko, he'd felt like a fraud. What he'd told Ming was true: he did have a lunch date with Kiko. The morning after speaking to the police, Andy had exchanged a series of text messages with her, in which they'd joked about all the mildly-offensive-and-possibly-racist things people had said to them over the years. Kiko had told Andy that people sometimes mistook her mum for the housekeeper. Andy told Kiko about his recent experience with the man on the tram. Kiko told Andy about all the men who'd shouted ni hao at her from passing cars. Andy told Kiko about the building manager on Spencer Street who'd got him mixed up

129

with the Korean accountant who lived ten floors down. It was surprisingly fun to share these experiences with someone who really understood them, and when Kiko said she had to go, Andy sent a message asking her again about the pho.

He studied the text messages now as he travelled home on the tram. The last message was one word: *yes*, with a single *x* for a kiss. Andy liked that one the best. He was so distracted he almost missed his stop, pressing the button at the very last minute. The tram lurched to a halt. On the brief walk home, Andy planned what he would wear to his post-exam date with Kiko. By the time he arrived at the house he had settled on black jeans and his Astro Boy T-shirt.

The sobbing was so loud, Andy could hear it from the front garden. It was different from the muffled cries he'd heard through Mrs Hughes' bedroom door a few weeks before. This was completely uncontrolled—it reminded Andy of his mother's wails as she was dragged from the house by ambulance officers. He found the old woman in the kitchen, slumped over a cup of tea.

'What's wrong?' Andy asked.

She looked up, her face crumpled. 'Atticus has gone.'

Andy's eyes found the empty cage.

'It's all my fault,' she said, burying her face in her hands. 'I was distracted. I've been so distracted lately—'

Andy wanted to ask how it had happened, but worried it would only distress her further.

'Where could he be?'

'I last saw him in the garden.'

Andy went outside. He'd arrived home later than usual, and the sun was setting. In this light even the untamed garden looked pretty—you could be forgiven for thinking the disorder was deliberate. He sat on the stone bench and searched the trees around him. Atticus was grey with a crimson tail. If he was there, he'd stand out amid all the green, and if they didn't see him, they would hear him—he was never quiet for very long.

Andy sat there, scanning the garden, but there was no sign of Atticus. For the sake of Mrs Hughes, who he assumed was listening from the kitchen, he called the parrot's name loudly a few times, but after ten minutes of looking, Andy knew in his heart that the bird was gone. He turned his attention instead to the sky—to the clouds, long and low and tinged with pink. He thought of Atticus and tried to imagine what it must be like to fly.

Ex-students had told Andy and Ming that on the aptitude test to get into medicine there'd once been a question asking candidates if they ever dreamt of flying. Ming had told Andy proudly that he dreamt about it all the time. Andy wondered what this particular detail revealed about a person's suitability for a career in medicine. Andy's recurring dreams were about turning up unprepared to an exam and standing naked in front of a crowd of girls—he'd never had a dream about flying. The closest he'd come was during his first flight to Australia, when he'd looked out through the cabin window at the red roofs and green lawns and blue pools and felt a certain freedom in his insignificance. Perhaps after thirty years in a cage, reciting nursery rhymes, Atticus wanted to feel that too.

After a reasonable amount of time had passed, Andy went back inside the house. Mrs Hughes looked at him with a hopeful face, but on seeing his empty hands she dropped her head.

'I'll put something on Facebook and Gumtree,' Andy said. She nodded.

'We'll find him,' he told her, resting a hand on her chair. He studied the dandruff scattered like snowflakes across the back of her blouse. 'Do you have a photo?'

As soon as he said it, Andy realised he could have used any photo of an African grey parrot from the internet—they all looked the same—but Mrs Hughes seemed grateful for something to do. She retreated to her room to search for a picture.

27

Meg pulled the shoeboxes of keepsakes out from under her bed. She couldn't remember the last time she'd taken a photo of Atticus, but she knew there would be one buried in there somewhere. She emptied the first box onto her bed. Photographs and receipts and letters spilt out across the bedspread. She picked up a black and white picture of her and Helen. It had been taken in summer and they were dressed in T-shirts and shorts. Helen was nearly as tall as her, even though Meg was five years older. Meg was stocky, like their father, with a barrel chest and a short neck, while Helen was lithe and athletic, her legs impossibly long. It was the only photo Meg had of Helen before her fall. After the accident their mother had hidden all the full-length pictures of her sister.

The shoeboxes were accidental time capsules. Over the years Meg had stuffed anything and everything inside them. She discovered two tickets to *West Side Story* at the Princess Theatre—a fortieth-birthday gift from Helen. She found her grade four report card, which said she was an intelligent but nervous child. She uncovered a necklace she and Helen had made from the shells they'd collected one Christmas holiday at Dromana. As she touched the shells, rolling each one between her fingers as if the chain was a kind of rosary, she felt an ache behind her breastbone. She was the only one left in the world who could make sense of these little treasures. Without her, they were rubbish—box after box of meaningless junk. She was a natural custodian—a keeper and guardian of things—but now, without anyone to share her memories, she began to question their accuracy. Was it really Safety Beach they had gone to? Had they really had prawns with thousand island dressing for lunch? Meg needed someone else—her mother, her father, Helen— to corroborate these memories and bring them back to life. Without her family, they were hazy, obscured by the cloudy lens of age.

She supposed somebody had to be the last to go. It made sense that it was her, but that didn't ease the loneliness. She'd been at all their bedsides—her mother, her father, Helen— and while there was peace in their faces at the end, all of them had squeezed her hand. Who or what would she squeeze as she lay, breathless, in her final hours? The clean, dry fingers of a nurse? The bedrail? The starched sheets of a hospital bed? Perhaps Jillian was right. Perhaps this isolation was of her own making. Maybe it was time she took control, became less passive and more active.

She packed away the necklace and the report card and resumed her search with renewed focus. This time she didn't permit herself distractions. Her concentration paid off—she found a photo of Atticus within minutes. She walked back to the kitchen and handed the photograph over to Andy, who was eating instant noodles beside the empty cage. When he was finished, he retreated to his room with promises to upload the image to the internet.

Meg packed the shoeboxes safely back beneath the bed. When she was done, she pulled her suitcase down from the top of her wardrobe. Untouched for decades, it was covered in what looked like a mix of cockroach poo and cobwebs. She set to work immediately, cleaning it with Windex and a sponge. The task was therapeutic—for a few brief moments she forgot about what Jillian had said. It was only once she started packing and caught sight of her limp clothes hanging in the cupboard that Meg felt the sting of her friend's words again. As she folded her navy blouses and black slacks, she understood that what people most craved in the world was often what they were most afraid of. For Meg, it was, and always had been, the attention of others.

Her mood lifted slightly at the discovery of one of Helen's old dresses—an emerald green sundress with tiny yellow flowers—which had been hiding for years on a hanger beneath a heavy coat. When she lifted the fabric to her nose she thought she could smell Helen's perfume amid the mustiness, but it must have been her imagination—she knew smells didn't last that long. Either way, she felt good when she put the dress on. Her sister had always been slimmer, but Meg had lost a couple of kilos in the past few months and the dress slipped on easily enough. If someone had been inclined to look, they might catch a glimpse of her bra where the fabric gaped between the buttons, but it didn't matter. The cheerful pattern brought some colour to her otherwise ashen face.

Anne had always maintained that a person could dress their way to happiness, but Meg wasn't so sure. She didn't believe you could create joy simply by throwing on a brightly coloured dress—she certainly couldn't shed her anxiety about Atticus like a pair of old slacks. But she did feel different wearing her sister's clothes—more confident and optimistic— as if she was less Meg and more Helen.

28

It was the night before the exam, and Andy was grateful for the distraction. He wouldn't have known how to occupy himself—it seemed senseless to study but also impossible to relax. He threw himself into the task of editing Atticus's photo. He played with filters, fiddled with the background, zoomed and cropped. Around eleven—aware that, while he worked on the image, someone could be identifying the missing bird—he uploaded the photo to Gumtree and a Facebook page called Lost Pets of Melbourne. Now he and Mrs Hughes could do nothing more but wait.

Andy turned off the light, but he wasn't tired. As he lay in bed, his mind raced. He thought of his mother. He tried to imagine her, watching television or pacing the halls of the hospital. Perhaps the doctor had given her a sedative and she was already fast asleep. Andy was terrified that one day he would shatter under the weight of his anxieties, as she had done. He couldn't help but wonder whether she'd still be the happy woman his father had married if she'd never fallen pregnant with him. Andy had only ever seen glimpses of that other woman over the years. There was one memory that stood out: the day he'd got a good mark on a big maths test. He'd been about eight—still in primary school. As a reward she'd taken him out for lunch, just the two of them. Andy had ordered a baked pork chop and iced lemon tea. His mother had put the exam paper—with its 98% scrawled in fat red pen at the top—on the table between them. As they ate, her smiling eyes had darted from the paper to Andy's face and back again, as if she couldn't quite believe his success. Andy had lived on that memory for years, calling it back every time she snapped at him, or called him an idiot, or yelled that she wished she'd never had him. He'd tried to convince himself that the woman smiling at him across the table that day was his real mother—not the person sitting on the couch with glassy eyes, barking orders at him.

Feeling his chest tighten, Andy forced himself to think of things other than his family. He turned his imagination to the boy who called himself Kanbei. What was he doing right now? Was he sleeping, brushing up on his microbiology or playing video games on his computer? The boy looked like a gamer—pale and unkempt and dressed in black from head to toe. Andy wondered what his story was. If Kanbei was so smart, why couldn't he find a better, more secure source of income? Was he on drugs? Did he have a huge gambling debt? But such thoughts weren't helping Andy to relax. He threw back the sheets and walked to the bathroom. He emptied his bladder, washed his hands and opened the mirrored cabinet above the basin. He kept his toiletries in his room—he'd never looked inside the cabinet before. The diazepam was sitting there on the middle shelf at eye height, its label turned outwards to face him.

Take one to two tablets half an hour prior to bedtime.

The label was more of an order than a suggestion. He felt like Alice in Wonderland—the book was one of the few English texts he'd studied at high school. The bottle may as well have said *Eat me.*

He opened the childproof lid: inside the bottle, there were twelve tablets left. Enough that Mrs Hughes probably wouldn't notice if one went missing. He popped a tablet, small as a Tic Tac, on his tongue and washed it down with a scoop of tap water. Immediately he felt calmer, his palms less sweaty, his heart rate slower. He knew this was the placebo effect—the medication had barely reached his stomach—but the change he felt was undeniable.

He lay on his bed as if on a cloud. As the benzodiazepine kicked in, he finally understood the lure of drugs. Up until then he had always thought of drug addicts as weak and out of control. Alcohol had never held any appeal for him, but this was different. There was no itch or heat, just a gentle soothing of his senses. Like exhaling after holding his breath for a really long time. Sleep came slowly. For half an hour he was caught in a kind of limbo. Instead of his mother and Kanbei,

his mind was awash with images of Kiko—the skin around
her eyes, which creased into fine wrinkles when she laughed,
her black hair burnished brown by the fierce Australian sun.

29

When the garbage truck roared past her window at six am, Meg woke up with a start. She rushed to the kitchen to see if Atticus might have magically returned during the night, but the kitchen and his cage were empty. She made a cup of tea, wrapped herself in a robe and stood on the front verandah to drink it. She hoped Atticus might be there, waiting patiently to be invited back in, but the street was deserted.

Her father had been an early riser—a hangover, perhaps, from being brought up on a farm. Sometimes when Meg was in her early teens, she'd set her alarm so she could sit with him as he drank his morning coffee in the garden. Meg always thought she took after her dad—a quiet and thoughtful man, easily overwhelmed by Helen and her mum. Bev and Judith were the only people on Rose Street old enough to remember him. There had been a time when Meg had prided herself on knowing the names of everyone on the street, but she'd given up trying years ago. Even Helen, who was always talking to strangers, had found it an impossible task in the end. Now there was a block of poky townhouses with a revolving door of new tenants. The people, young professionals mainly, were friendly, but always in such a rush.

Meg forced herself to focus on the day ahead. She wished she could be more like Patrick—spirited and passionate—but she only felt sad and weary. Even now, as she stood on the verandah, her belly ached and her knees throbbed. Tired, she sat down on the steps of the porch. The bleeding had settled a few days ago, which she assumed was a good sign. She put down her mug and rubbed her stomach, scanning the trees for a flash of red. But apart from a plastic bag tied to a branch—which momentarily set Meg's heart aflutter—there was nothing.

30

Andy woke up late, feeling refreshed. There was nowhere he had to be and he lay in bed for fifteen minutes. When he eventually checked his phone he saw there were three missed calls from an unknown number. At three am the caller had left a voicemail message.

'This is Kanbei. I've got food poisoning. I can't go today. Don't worry about the outstanding balance. I'll only keep the non-refundable fifty per cent deposit.'

Andy sat up in bed. The exam had started at nine o'clock. He checked the time on his phone—it was ten-thirty. He felt a wash of panic. A thousand thoughts flooded his head. What would his parents say when they found out? Failing was shameful, but cheating on an exam was unforgivable.

Perhaps this would be the thing that would push his mother over the edge. Had he really expected a criminal to honour a verbal contract? Served him right. He'd got what was coming to him. He'd got what he deserved.

Feeling as though he might faint, Andy lay down again. He grabbed the edge of the bed in an attempt to anchor himself in the world. What was it the counsellor at uni had taught him during their first session? Three things he could feel, three things he could hear. He could feel the pillow beneath his head, the wooden bedframe in his hand, his hair resting on his forehead. He could hear a motorbike storming past the house, the distant cry of a child, birds chirping outside the window. He concentrated on his breathing. He counted to three as he inhaled, three as he exhaled. He closed his eyes. Nobody knew anything yet. Three things he could feel, three things he could hear. He could feel the tension in his muscles, the pound of his pulse in his temples, the air moving through his nostrils. He could hear a piano, a bicycle bell, a tree branch tapping on the window. What if he got an appointment with a doctor and faked the food poisoning Kanbei was supposedly suffering from? He imagined people got medical certificates from doctors to explain their absence from exams all the time. Andy opened his laptop and searched for clinics in the area. He found one not far away, along a tramline. When he called, the receptionist said he was in luck and gave him an appointment for eleven-thirty. He could see the doctor and still see Kiko at one o'clock like they'd planned. He would have to sit a supplementary exam, but at least it would give him more time to study.

Andy tried calling the number Kanbei had given him. He rang it five times, but there was no answer. He felt a hollowness invade his abdomen—something akin to hunger but much more painful. He didn't even know Kanbei's real name.

Andy walked to the kitchen, relieved to discover that Mrs Hughes wasn't at home. He wondered whether she'd gone in search of Atticus, or if perhaps she was on another date with her racist boyfriend. Either way, Andy was grateful for the silence. He made a coffee and placed the mug beside his books on the kitchen table. He had thirty minutes to study for the neuroscience exam before he'd have to leave for his appointment with the GP. But as he leafed through the course handbook and scoured the relevant chapters in his textbook, he was daunted by the task ahead of him. At eleven, when his father sent him a message asking how he'd gone in his exam, Andy shoved his books to the floor and ran to the bathroom to douse his face with water. Now he sat on the lid of the toilet and concentrated on his breathing. A certificate wasn't going to solve everything, but it was definitely better than nothing. This thought momentarily calmed him and he got dressed to see the doctor. Before he left, he tidied up the mess he'd made in the kitchen. Mrs Hughes had enough problems of her own—she didn't need an untidy housemate.

The clinic was three blocks from the house, in what had once been a family home. In the waiting room Andy pretended to read a magazine about cars while he studied the other patients. There was a snotty toddler stuffing sultanas into his mouth on the chair directly opposite, and an old man with a hacking cough on the seat beside him.

At eleven forty-five, the doctor—a middle-aged man with a large belly—called out Andy's name. Andy followed him down the hall. The GP was breathless by the time they reached the room. As he sat down, Andy's eyes found a CT scan report at the top of a messy pile of papers. Herman Pickford. Sixty-seven years old. Metastatic lung cancer.

'So,' the doctor said, swivelling round in his chair. He squinted at the computer screen. 'Andy. Chan. What can I help you with today?'

Andy wrapped his arm around his abdomen and bent forwards. 'I think I've got food poisoning.'

The doctor picked up the clipboard with the questionnaire Andy had filled out in the waiting room. 'You're studying biomedicine?'

Andy nodded. He was hoping this detail would make the doctor more sympathetic. 'I've actually got an exam today. Microbiology.'

'In which case you can tell me which two bacterial toxins are most commonly responsible for food poisoning.'

Andy's fingers gripped the sides of the chair.

The doctor laughed. 'I'm just pulling your leg.' He spun around to face the computer screen. 'I suppose you're after a medical certificate.'

On the brief walk to the clinic Andy had perfected his story. He'd woken up at three am with projectile vomiting and hadn't been able to tolerate anything but small sips of water since. This morning he'd had three episodes of watery diarrhoea with no blood. He thought it was probably the sushi he'd eaten yesterday for lunch. But the doctor didn't ask him any questions. Either he was a very bad doctor who didn't examine his patients, or he was a very good doctor who saw through Andy's performance.

The printer on the desk shuddered to life. The doctor removed a piece of paper from its mouth and handed it to Andy. It was a medical certificate for one day.

'You should be right by tomorrow,' the doctor said with an amused look on his face. 'If it's really just food poisoning.'

31

Patrick arrived at one o'clock. On the phone he'd told Meg that check-in at the beach house was three pm. Meg had spent the morning visiting the neighbours for news about Atticus, but nobody had seen him.

'Have you been to Dromana before?' Patrick asked when they were packed and seated in the car.

'A few times, with the family, when I was a little girl.' Meg thought of the shell necklace she'd stuffed back into the shoebox last night. She hoped she hadn't damaged it.

'It's a great spot.'

Patrick was casually dressed in a polo shirt, shorts and sandals. Instead of a leather cap, his balding head was covered by a fedora.

Meg leant back in her seat. She'd never taken much interest in cars, but she could tell this one was expensive, probably European. Not big but spacious, with tan leather seats.

'This car has seat warmers. Not that we need them today.'

Meg raised her eyebrows. She hadn't realised the world had progressed to the point of seat warmers. If anything, she'd always found it a little disconcerting to sit on a chair that was still hot from another person's bottom. But she supposed it was different if a computer had heated it for you.

'I remember when the only way to cool a car was to open a window,' she said.

Patrick laughed. 'Those days are over.'

Meg looked at him, unsure if he was sad or excited about the future.

'In a few years we'll have cars that don't even need a driver,' he added.

Meg had heard about such things on the radio. 'It's hard to believe.'

Patrick chuckled. 'If you're rich enough, soon you'll be able to do almost everything with the press of a button.'

Meg thought of Helen with her useless legs. Now people with perfectly good legs were developing technology to ensure they'd never have to use them. She thought of the daytime telly advertisements for whole-body vibrators designed to help people lose weight while they sat on the couch and watched more daytime telly advertisements for whole-body vibrators.

'I've packed a picnic,' Patrick said. 'Tasmanian brie, homemade parmesan crisps and marinated Sicilian olives.'

'Sounds delicious.' It struck Meg that her recent meal of

spaghetti bolognese must have seemed terribly pedestrian to Patrick. She looked out the window. They were driving past the Melbourne cemetery. A large billboard mounted to the wrought-iron fence read: *Limited release! Exclusive graves. A once-in-a-lifetime opportunity.*

As they waited at the traffic light, Meg saw a flash of emerald and blue in a nearby gum tree. Taking a closer look, she realised a small flock of rainbow lorikeets had made their home in its branches. She turned to Patrick, who was tapping his fingers on the steering wheel. The radio was tuned to Gold FM. Marvin Gaye's 'I Heard It through the Grapevine' was playing. There was something about his look, a smugness, that Meg found unnerving. She felt a sharp pain in her chest. When she inhaled, the air was as thick as honey.

'Do you mind opening a window?' she gasped.

'Are you okay?' Patrick said as he pulled over.

'I can't do this.' As she spoke Meg thought she saw a flicker of irritation pass across his face. 'Atticus, he's flown away,' she said.

'I'm sorry.' Patrick placed a warm hand on Meg's arm.

A skinny woman walking a dalmatian peered at them through the windscreen.

'I know it sounds pathetic,' Meg said. 'But he's been with me a long time.'

'Of course.' Patrick's hand slipped down Meg's arm towards her wrist. He turned her hand palm up and interlaced his fingers with hers. 'But what good will it do to wait for him at home?'

'I want to be there when he comes back,' Meg said, imagining Jillian's sneer.

'Don't Worry, Be Happy' was now playing on the radio. Patrick turned it off. 'Have you ever thought that maybe Atticus isn't lost at all? That maybe he's enjoying his new-found freedom?'

Meg knew he was talking about her, but as she sat in the airless cabin of the car, her seatbelt tight as a noose around her neck, she felt anything but free.

32

On the tram Andy tried to focus on his meeting with Kiko. Now he wouldn't have to lie about being at the exam today. He could tell her a new version of events—one that didn't involve so much diarrhoea, something along the lines of his alarm not going off—and, even better, ask her about the exam questions.

He watched a couple standing by the tram doors, kissing and whispering. People pretended to look at their phones, but every so often Andy saw their eyes flick up towards the lovers. He was relieved when the tram arrived at his stop. He squeezed past the couple and the woman smiled at him, her lipstick so smeared it was hard to tell where her lips began and where they ended.

Andy chose a quiet table at the back of the restaurant. It was still five weeks until Christmas but somebody had strung red and silver tinsel across the ceiling. As one o'clock neared, Andy could sense every muscle in his body tighten.

'Can I take your order?' the waitress asked with an impatient look. It was the third time she had asked him.

'I'll wait for my friend,' Andy replied.

By one-thirty, Andy must have checked his phone sixty times, but there were no messages from Kiko. When he waved down the waitress and ordered beef pho, he thought he saw an annoying I-told-you-so smile on her lips. He ate slowly, partly to justify his continued presence and partly because each bite was an effort. When he finished eating it was past two o'clock and Andy had to accept what the waitress had been so sure of from the start—Kiko wasn't coming. He contemplated messaging her—perhaps she'd been mugged or murdered as she walked from the exam hall to meet him. Perhaps she was dead or dying a slow death in a dumpster somewhere. Perhaps it was all his fault. Or maybe she'd just stood him up. As hard as it was to admit, Andy knew the last option was the most likely. There was nothing he could do. His parents had raised him to preserve face—he couldn't message a girl after she'd humiliated him.

The air inside the tram was stifling. No matter where Andy sat, he couldn't escape the smell of body odour. There was no kissing couple this time, only a man with leaves in his hair talking loudly to an invisible companion.

Andy had had an imaginary friend as a child. He'd never

told his parents about him. He'd worried it would make them angry, or sad, or both. But he remembered his make-believe companion—an older and braver version of himself—rolling his eyes at the noisy way his dad ate and making funny faces behind his mother's back as she fussed about the kitchen.

The tram rumbled up Swanston Street and came to a stop at a busy intersection. The man with leaves in his hair got off and a group of university students climbed on. They were chatting loudly about an exam, complaining about the poorly worded questions. Andy slumped down in his seat, leant his head against the window.

He didn't recognise his aunt straight away. She was wearing a white shirt with lace sleeves and bright red lipstick. She looked younger and prettier than usual. She was sitting at an outside table beneath an awning, having coffee with a man. As the tram started moving again Andy's thoughts turned to his birthday. He remembered the excuses his aunt had made when he'd suggested they meet for yum cha—the school pick-ups, the distance, the kids' sporting activities. No wonder Kiko couldn't face having lunch with him—even his own family found him boring.

When Andy arrived home, Atticus was perched on the letterbox, scratching his belly with his beak. Andy smiled, less surprised by the return of the parrot than by how moved he felt.

Atticus bobbed his head up and down. 'Humpty Dumpty sat on a wall!'

Andy held out his hand and the parrot climbed onto it. As

Andy fumbled with the key, Atticus whistled a tune. They went inside together.

Mrs Hughes wasn't home. Andy couldn't bring himself to put Atticus back in his cage. He didn't want to imprison the bird after his recent bout of freedom. Instead he let the parrot roam free around the house.

At the sight of his neuroscience textbooks on the kitchen table, Andy felt a hole open up inside his chest. He called Kanbei three times, but every time it rang through to voicemail. On the third call he left an angry message about verbal contracts and the natural history of food poisoning.

Enraged, Andy paced up and down the hallway. Atticus chased him, which only infuriated Andy more. He paused outside the bathroom. Mrs Hughes had left the cabinet slightly ajar. Andy went in, ignoring his frantic face in the mirror as he opened the cabinet door. Atticus didn't follow, preferring to watch at a safe distance from the floor of the hall.

Andy picked up the bottle and pushed down on the childproof lid with his palm. He only wanted to sleep, to quell the noises in his head, to take a break from the exhaustion of being himself. The tablets fell like lollies onto his tongue. He filled his mouth with water from the tap and sat on the toilet seat to wait.

33

Meg stepped out of the car into the heat. They hadn't moved from the spot where Patrick had pulled over, next to the cemetery.

'Are you sure you'll be okay?' Patrick said as he unloaded her bag from the boot.

'I'll be fine,' Meg said, taking the suitcase. 'You should keep going, enjoy the beach.'

Patrick had offered countless times to drive her home, but Meg had politely refused. Even the most excruciating pain was preferable to another minute with him inside the car. If she saw a taxi or a tram she would catch it. Until then she would walk, resting at park benches and tram stops along the way. This was the route she had taken when she was working—and having sex—with Tim. Back then she had walked with long strides and proud shoulders—her neck tingling from the bristle of Tim's kisses, her body alight with the memory of his touch. Meg wondered what her younger self would say to her now. What would she have made of this dramatic escape from a handsome man who wanted to be with her?

Her legs ached. The suitcase had wheels, but the handle dug into her palm. She was walking alongside the gates of the cemetery, and without thinking she wandered inside, searching for a spot to rest. Her father had brought her and Helen to the cemetery once—he'd said it would be a good lesson in history. Their mother had scolded him for taking them, describing it as creepy and morbid, but Meg and Helen had enjoyed the visit, reading the names on the tombstones and taking turns to scare each other with ghost stories about the dead.

Walking through the cemetery sixty years later, Meg couldn't have had a more different experience. Death was something she thought about every day now. She didn't look at tombstones and think of horror films; she thought of people—mothers and fathers, sons and daughters, colleagues and friends. She took care to read the inscriptions, to whisper the names, to imagine these people and how they'd died. Even the oldest graves, their headstones rendered nameless by the wash of countless storms, captured her imagination.

Near the west gate she found the headstone of a woman who shared the same birthday as her. She sat down on the small square patch of weeds beside it. The woman's name was

Maria, and she'd died three years ago, aged seventy-two. She was Italian, buried with her husband beneath a grand, gold-flecked slab. It was one of the only graves with fresh flowers—a pretty bouquet of pink carnations and baby's breath—laid upon it. Meg had had an Italian friend at high school called Cristina. She'd had five siblings and was always complaining about being dragged to family gatherings on the weekends—weddings and birthdays, christenings and confirmations.

Apart from Christmas, Meg and her family didn't have get-togethers. Her mother's family were scattered across New South Wales, South Australia and the UK, while her father had cut all ties with his relatives. Meg's parents had brought her up to believe that extended family brought only problems—her mother's anxiety in the lead-up to Christmas and her relief on seeing her aunt's car recede into the distance after lunch only served to reinforce this. But now Meg wondered if she wouldn't have been better off with European parents. A traditional mother and father who had forced her to marry into another large, loud European family. Maybe then she wouldn't be sitting in a cemetery, alone, the only surviving member of her clan, staring at another woman's gravestone.

The sun was high overhead. Meg looked at her watch. She'd lost more than an hour wandering through the cemetery. Above her a flock of rainbow lorikeets shrieked, a splash of colour across the grey clouds. She thought of Atticus. Perhaps Patrick was right. Perhaps he'd found happiness now. She'd always felt a pang of guilt when she hooked the latch on his cage. Surely human beings had always been jealous of birds' ability to silently soar across the sky. She stood up, felt the pull of gravity on her bones.

Just before she reached the gate, she caught a glimpse of a headstone, broken in two, beneath her dusty feet. The earth had consumed most of it, but she could still make out the words of the faded engraving: *Until the day breaks and the shadows flee.*

As she left the cemetery, she was relieved to see a taxi dropping off a passenger a few metres from the gate.

The driver wound down the window. 'You after a taxi?'

'Yes, please,' Meg said, feeling faint. She deposited the suitcase in the boot, climbed into the front seat and put on her seatbelt. She told the driver her address. There was a photo of him on the dashboard. His name was Ali.

'You okay?' he asked.

Meg leant back against the headrest and closed her eyes. 'Better, now.'

'Lady your age shouldn't be walking on such a hot day.'

'I know.' Meg felt like a child being scolded. Ali must have sensed this, because when he spoke again his voice was softer.

'Were you visiting someone?' he said, and when Meg seemed confused, he added, 'At the *cemetery*?' He whispered the word as if it was a curse.

'Oh, no,' Meg said, and shook her head. She supposed he must have thought it strange for an old woman to be wandering aimlessly through a cemetery. 'I just needed somewhere to rest my feet.'

'Would you like some water?' Ali asked. 'You look like you need some water. I think I have a bottle in the back.' He alternated his gaze between her and the road.

'I'm fine.' Meg stopped short of explaining that this was just how she looked—wrinkled and desiccated. No amount of water was going to help her. 'How old do you think I am?'

Ali waved his finger in the air and smiled. 'I know this is a trick question!'

'No, really, I want to know.'

Ali shook his head. 'The only correct answer to that question is twenty-one. The most beautiful age for everyone.'

Meg thought of Andy with his acne scars and sad eyes. She wondered if he knew he'd never be more beautiful than he was now.

Meg said goodbye to Ali and walked the few steps to her house with a proud, taut back, conscious of him watching her with concern in his big brown eyes. When he had driven off, she surrendered to the pain and leant against the front door, her legs burning. The pounding in her head eased as her key found the lock, but it started up again at the sound of a high-pitched shriek from behind the door. Atticus? But how had he got inside? Had she left a window open? Or had she only imagined the noise?

She left the suitcase by the door and followed the white patches of poo like tiny stepping stones across the floorboards. They led her to the kitchen, where she found Atticus on the table, preening himself amid the spilt contents of a cornflakes box. He stopped his grooming to look at her. Meg felt all the emotion of the day's events suddenly seize her. She collapsed in a chair, in a fit of tears. Atticus fluffed his feathers, and she held out her arm to him.

'Humpty Dumpty sat on a wall! Humpty Dumpty had a great fall!' the parrot sang, before making a long whistling noise.

Meg recalled a newspaper article she'd read once about a prisoner who was so accustomed to jail he'd committed crime after crime to be locked up again. She wondered if that was why Atticus had come back to her—he'd grown so used to living in a cage he didn't know how to do anything else. She hoped not. She prayed he was just an introvert like her—overwhelmed by the big, brutal, beautiful world.

Meg tidied up the kitchen and made herself a cup of tea. She should feel relieved, or happy, but if anything she felt uneasy. It didn't help that Atticus wouldn't stop singing 'Humpty Dumpty'. When she couldn't stand it anymore, she put him in his cage and threw the sheet over him. Perhaps he was sleep-deprived or over-stimulated after his recent adventure, like a child.

She retreated to the bedroom. It was afternoon, and a yolky light oozed through a gap between the curtains, bathing everything in an orange glow. She rested on her bed for ten minutes before getting up to use the toilet. Through the half-open bathroom door she saw that the cabinet above the sink was open and her medicine bottles were strewn across the floor. She thought of Atticus and opened the door.

Meg didn't see Andy straight away. He'd fallen into the space between the toilet and the bath, his arms sticking out at awkward angles. On seeing him, she fell to her knees.

A million thoughts raced through her head. Andy's mother and father—she had no way of contacting them. Would the agency blame her for leaving her medications within easy reach? Andy was officially an adult, but with his hairless skin and beseeching eyes, he often looked more like a child. She should have taken greater care with him!

She could hardly see his face, slouched behind the toilet. She thought for sure he must be dead, but when she touched his arm it was still warm, and if she listened carefully she could hear a quiet gurgle coming from his mouth. She tried to remember what she'd been taught at a first-aid class she'd attended years ago. The ABCs, they'd called it, but God knew what they stood for. Instinct told her she should extricate him from between the toilet and the bath. It was hard work, but somehow she managed to pull him out. Every few seconds Meg heard the reassuring warble of his breath, but in between times his chest barely seemed to rise. Finally it occurred to her to call for help. She found her purse and dialled 000 on her phone.

Meg stood in the hallway with her back to the wall, watching the paramedics at work. Atticus, who had refused to settle in his cage, watched them too. She felt envious of their knowledge of the human body—the way they reduced flesh and blood to simple mechanics. She watched them flash lights into Andy's eyes and inspect his arms for needle marks. There was something beautiful about the way they moved around his body in a perfectly coordinated dance, not once bumping hands or reaching for the same instrument, not once getting in each other's way. For the most part they even managed to ignore Atticus's calls for attention—only exchanging a smile when the exasperated bird screamed, 'How rude!'

Meg understood that Andy was alive, but only just. The medicine had made his airway floppy and he was at risk of choking on his own tongue. She'd heard the lady paramedic say that if Meg had arrived ten minutes later, they might not have been able to save him. As the paramedic spoke, Meg recalled that the A in ABC stood for airway. It had taken her over half an hour to remember this—fat lot of good she was in an emergency.

The house was quiet, eerily so. Atticus, sick of being ignored, had gone back to his cage in a huff. At one point, the lady paramedic forgot the brakes on the stretcher and it momentarily rolled away from her. She said, 'Sorry, Max,' and Max said, 'No worries,' as if they were in a café and she'd accidentally bumped his coffee.

When ambulance officers had first visited the house, on the day of Helen's accident, the place hadn't been nearly so quiet. The air had resonated for what seemed like days with her mother's screams and Helen's unanswered questions: 'Why can't I feel my legs? Why can't I wriggle my toes?'

'Would you like to travel with him? In the back of the ambulance?' the lady paramedic asked Meg.

Meg imagined Andy waking up along the way, a plastic mask over his face and a plastic tube hanging from his arm. The lady paramedic was pretty, angelic even, but she was still a stranger. Meg and Andy might not be friends, but they were definitely more than strangers.

The ambulance officers helped Meg into the back of the vehicle, which sat surprisingly high above the ground. As they drove, the lady paramedic, who introduced herself as Sharon, told Meg she could hold Andy's hand. Meg looked at Andy, his skin sallow, his cheeks sunken. She was quite sure he wouldn't know if she was holding his hand or not, but she didn't want Sharon to think her unkind. She placed her fingers lightly on his arm and felt the thrill of his pulse beneath his skin.

34

It's hot. The air conditioner is broken. Andy's mother is sitting in front of the only fan in the house, watching Cantonese soap operas. Andy has been banished to his bedroom for calling his mother a smelly cunt. Really it was the voice in his mother's head that swore at her, but she's so deep into her sickness that facts have become irrelevant. Andy's father is in China—a rich man in Shenzhen is interested in investing in his cleaning business. Before he left, he gave Andy a list of emergency phone numbers, but Andy is locked in his bedroom and the phone is in the lounge room.

He writes a note—*My mum is hearing voices and she's locked me in my room*—and throws it through the bars of the bedroom window. He watches it float down and come to rest on top of an air-conditioning unit. A pigeon pecks at it briefly before flying away. It's at times like this that Andy wishes he had a sibling—someone to reassure him that it is in fact his mother, and not him, who is unwell. His granddad was good at doing this before he died, but now, alone with his thoughts, Andy starts to wonder if perhaps he did call his mother a smelly cunt—God knows he's thought the words in his head enough times.

He looks at the Astro Boy figurine on his desk—a recent present from his father. In the Japanese manga series, Astro Boy was created by a scientist to replace his dead son, Tobio. The scientist eventually rejected the robot on realising that, while the android looked like his son, and had all of Tobio's memories, he was incapable of expressing emotion like a normal human child.

As Andy thinks these things he feels the soles of his feet begin to burn. When he sits down on his bed to inspect them, he sees they're glowing red like hot coals. The noises from the street, twenty storeys below, grow louder. He can hear pigeons' coos as if the birds are right next to his ear. He walks to the bedroom door and turns the knob. There's a slight resistance before it swings open. His mother turns to look at him, a wet face towel on her forehead. She smiles and suddenly she isn't his mother anymore, she's Kiko—kind, gentle Kiko. Andy feels her soft fingers on his arm before the apartment block that has been his home since he was born unfolds like a piece of origami. Then the floor, too, falls away, leaving Andy suspended. Flames shoot from the soles of his feet. He is flying.

35

There were no lights or sirens when Helen was taken to hospital for the last time. In the weeks leading up to her death, she'd been battling an infected pressure sore and everybody had just assumed her fever was caused by her wound. In fact she'd developed pneumonia from lying in bed for so long. By the time it was picked up, Helen had a lung full of pus. The doctor, a straightforward fellow, had said she might not last the night. When Helen was transferred to hospital, Meg had followed the ambulance in her car. The paramedics had driven slowly, or so it felt to Meg, and it had upset her, because every minute on the road was a minute less spent at Helen's bedside.

Today the paramedics weaved their way across tramlines to get to the emergency department in good time. When they arrived, there were people in blue scrubs and gloves waiting to greet them. Sharon barked numbers at the doctors in an urgent way that reminded Meg of the doctor shows she watched sometimes on TV. It made Meg wonder whether young people's lives were held more dear because they had more life to lose. She recalled a nurse at the hospital telling her that Helen had had a good innings. At the time Meg had wanted to ask what defined a good innings. Was a good innings for an able-bodied mother of five different from that for a paraplegic woman with no kids? Nothing annoyed Meg more than platitudes—the funeral had been rife with them. *She's at peace now. It was her time. God needed another angel.* As far as Meg could tell, people only said these things to fill the silence and make themselves feel better. The truth was, Helen had loved life and was terrified of dying. Meg knew this because Helen had told her so, almost every day.

The doctors asked Meg to fill out Andy's forms. There were a lot of questions she couldn't answer. Things like emergency contacts and next of kin. She would, she knew, have to notify the agency—it was only a matter of time—but she wanted to wait until she had a better idea of Andy's prognosis. She wanted to be able to temper any anger or disapproval with reassurance that Andy was going to be okay. Out of the corner of her eye she saw a young man in a red T-shirt smiling at her. He had brown skin and brown eyes and his shirt said *Ask Me.* When Meg made eye contact he immediately walked towards her.

'Hi, my name's Ash—I'm a hospital volunteer. Can I help you?'

Meg shook her head. 'I don't think so.'

'Something to drink perhaps?' He spoke in a deliberate and thoughtful way, not rushing or swallowing his words like a native English speaker.

'Really?' Some of the other patients in the waiting room looked over in their direction with surprised faces.

'Water, orange juice, tea…'

'I'd love a cup of tea.'

Ash disappeared and re-emerged a few minutes later with a polystyrene cup. Meg took it from him. She looked at the label on the tea bag that simply read BLACK TEA. When she held the cup to her nose the hot liquid had no smell.

'Is there anything else I can do for you?'

'No thank you,' Meg replied, but Ash sat down on the plastic seat beside her.

'Have you been waiting long?'

She realised he'd mistaken her for a patient. 'I'm not sick. I'm here with someone.' Meg looked at the boy's smooth face. He couldn't be much older than Andy. She wondered why he spent his spare time doing this, what he got out of it.

'A relative?'

'Yes,' she lied, not wanting to explain her relationship to Andy.

'They will take good care of him,' Ash said, and then paused as if something had occurred to him. 'Is it a *him*?'

Meg nodded. She knew the boy would assume she was waiting for her husband. 'And what about you?' she said, keen to change the subject. 'What brings you to volunteer in an emergency department?'

'I like talking to people.'

Neither of them spoke for a few minutes after that. Meg surveyed the waiting room. Some people were sleeping on beds created from jackets thrown over plastic seats. Others were staring blankly at the floor. Most were occupied with their phones, swiping their fingers across the screens in a mechanical fashion.

'I've learnt to speak Australian English in this waiting room,' Ash said. 'I've learnt a couple of words in Italian, Arabic and Mandarin too.'

Meg looked at the boy's thick lashes and brown skin. Curious, she asked, 'Is Ash short for something?'

'Ashmal. It means perfect.' Ash waved a hand over his face. 'I'm Indian.'

She wondered if he'd chosen the anglicised nickname or if it had been chosen for him. 'I'm Margaret,' she said. 'A friend told me it means pearl.'

Ashmal's face lit up. 'I love pearls. I'm doing honours in zoology at university. Molluscs are my specialty.'

Meg smiled, fascinated by this young man whose interests included molluscs and talking to people.

'Do you know how pearls are formed?' he asked, sitting up.

Of course she did, but she shook her head—he seemed so thrilled at the prospect of educating her.

'It all starts with a foreign body. A parasite, a bit of grit. The mollusc creates a layer of cells around the intruder, which eventually calcifies to form the pearl.' Ashmal's eyes glistened as he spoke.

'That's amazing,' she said.

'Isn't it? Something so beautiful from something so small and accidental.'

Just then Meg heard a nurse call her name. Flustered, she stood up and walked off. It was only when she reached the nurse that she realised she'd forgotten to say goodbye to Ashmal. She turned to wave, but when she glanced back through the double doors he was already chatting to somebody else.

The nurse ushered Meg into a small room with a painting of yellow tulips on the wall. She pointed to a couch beneath the painting and Meg sat down.

'Can I get you something? A cup of tea?'

'No thanks.' Meg couldn't remember the hospital staff being so forthcoming with hot beverages when her mother was dying. Perhaps this was a new thing—a cheap and easy way of improving scores on some annual hospital survey.

The nurse regarded her with sympathetic eyes. 'I'll get one of the doctors.'

Meg had spent time in these 'family rooms' before. They were horrible places—a kind of badly furnished limbo. She braced herself for the worst.

When the doctor arrived, he looked about Andy's age, but was probably much older. By then Meg was feeling steely. She listened politely to the doctor's preamble. He was like a taller and more confident version of Andy. His voice was steady, but there were tiny beads of sweat on his upper lip. She wondered if this was the first time he'd had to break bad news to a patient. She imagined a senior doctor sending him forth with a militant slap on the back—a young soldier on a mission.

'We gave him something to reverse the effects of the overdose. But he's still very sedated. And we're running some tests on his lungs. He's been a little difficult to ventilate.'

Meg exhaled. Andy was alive.

'What I wanted to clarify with you, Mrs Hughes, is Andy's home situation.'

'He rents a room in my home. I'm the owner.'

'And do you know anything about his family?'

'The agency handles all that.'

'And do you have the details of the agency?'

Meg pulled her wallet from her handbag. She found the agency's business card and handed it to the doctor. As she did so, she felt a tremendous relief, both that Andy was alive and that she wouldn't have to call the agency herself.

The doctor scribbled the phone number on his clipboard. He seemed more relaxed too, perhaps pleased that his task was nearly complete. 'Do you have any questions?'

'What do you mean, difficult to ventilate?'

The doctor's smooth brow became furrowed again. 'I mean that we're needing to use greater pressure than normal to inflate Andy's lungs. As I said, we're running some tests. Hopefully it's nothing.'

Meg smiled. She didn't believe the doctor, but she wanted to relieve him of his misery.

•

The agency was called. A representative would be sent out to assess the situation straight away. At a later date they would arrange a meeting with Meg at home. Meg sat with Andy in the ICU. The bed was so high and the chair was so low, all she could see was Andy's unmoving hand on top of the sheets. After half an hour the nurse told her to go and have a cup of tea. Meg was thankful. Ever since the discussion in the family room she'd been waiting for permission to leave—to eat, to rest, to use the toilet. She supposed ICU nurses, used to seeing people reduced to hapless shells of their former selves, were trained to sense such things.

Meg followed the nurse, whose name was Jacky, to the tearoom. She nibbled the ice-cold cheese sandwich Jacky fetched for her from the fridge. She drank the mug of hot tea Jacky poured her from the kettle. It felt good to be looked after. So good, in fact, she felt her eyes prick with tears. She supposed she'd been looking for that kind of care when she'd signed up to the homeshare program, but now she realised Andy was just a child, too unwell to help himself, let alone her.

'Thank you,' Meg said.

Jacky smiled above the brim of her mug. 'I should thank you. I'd normally be smoking on my tea-break—you're effectively saving my life.'

Meg laughed.

'I suppose you think I'm terrible,' Jacky said.

'Not at all.'

'The thing is, working here, seeing all the things I see... it makes me want to take what little pleasures I can get.'

Meg looked at the nurse. She must have been in her late twenties. She had clear skin and straight teeth.

'But I will quit,' Jacky said. 'For my three-year-old son. He's got asthma.'

Meg felt her eyelids grow heavy. She stood up, brushed her skirt with her hands, hitched her handbag onto her shoulder.

'I'll be back tomorrow.'

'We'll call you if anything changes.'

'Please do.'

As Meg walked through the door she felt the nurse's fingers like an iron clamp on her wrist.

'You're bleeding.'

Meg turned around. She followed the nurse's eyes to the seat of her chair. Suddenly she was in second form again and her period had arrived a week early. It was Jillian who had saved her then, fetching a spare skirt from lost property.

'I'm so sorry,' Meg said and searched her purse for a tissue.

'Don't worry about cleaning up,' Jacky said, and loosened her grip. 'I'll take you down to emergency.'

'Oh, no. That won't be necessary. It's all being sorted by my doctor. I have an appointment for my test results next Monday.' The lies slipped out fast and easy. She watched the nurse's pretty face relax into a smile.

'Make sure you get plenty of rest. Eat lots of things with iron.'

The sun was rising when Meg got home. She jumped straight into the shower. Thankfully there was no more bleeding. She felt an ache, like period pain, above her pubic bone. After her shower she lay on her bed, relieved to be off her feet. It had been years since she'd done so much walking, and she was surprised her knees weren't more painful. She supposed it was all the adrenaline pumping like a wonder drug through her body. She could feel it now, keeping her awake, making her heart beat violently. As she lay there she heard a noise like a hand drill coming from Andy's bedroom. Atticus must have heard it too—he screeched.

She found the vibrating phone just in time to press the green button.

'Hello?' she said.

There was a mumble and a cough. 'Uh, sorry, wrong number.'

'Are you looking for Andy?'

'Yes?'

'Are you a friend of his?'

There was a long pause. 'Who is this? And why have you got Andy's mobile?'

'I'm Margaret Hughes. The woman he lives with.'

Another pause. Meg could hear the rumble of a tram, people talking.

'Is Andy okay?' asked the voice at the other end of the line.

'He will be. But he's in hospital.'

'Shit!' More talking in the background. 'Sorry, miss.'

'That's okay. I can give you the details of the hospital if you want to visit him.'

'What happened?'

'I can tell you more at the hospital. The main thing is that he's okay. Do you know if anything might've been troubling him? Anything with university or his family?'

'No. I mean, I don't know. There's this girl, her name's Kiko, I think he likes her. I don't know anything about his family.'

'Never mind.'

'I should have asked him.'

Meg detected a change in the stranger's voice. It had been brusque when she'd first picked up the phone; now it was gentle, apologetic.

'I should have too,' she said.

36

There were beeps, low-pitched and regular. His tongue felt like a fat piece of cloth inside his mouth. He moved his lips to speak but, hard as he tried, he couldn't utter a sound. When he opened his eyes, the light was blinding and he had to close them again. He felt movement at his elbow. When the woman spoke her voice was muffled, as if he was submerged under water.

'He's rousing.'

He could feel fingers, light and warm, on his arm. He tried his eyes again. A white face in a haze of light.

'Andy? Can you hear me?'

He mouthed the word for water and almost immediately felt a plastic straw on his lower lip. The thirst was intense and overwhelming. He drank greedily.

The woman laughed. 'Anyone would think you hadn't drunk for weeks!'

Andy licked his lips. He looked around him. The world was screened on three sides by pale blue curtains. At the foot of the bed a woman in scrubs was scribbling something on a chart.

'How long have I been here?' Andy asked, sounding out each syllable slowly, like a child.

'Two days and two nights. One here in ICU. One in emergency.'

Andy remembered the tablets. More than anything he felt embarrassed. He ran his hand—the one that wasn't hooked up to a bag of fluid—along his thigh. He was naked except for a gown. Thoughts tumbled, unbidden, into his brain. He thought of Kiko, of Mrs Hughes, of Ming. He thought of the agency, his parents, the university. Did anyone know what had happened—and if they knew, how much did they know? Exhausted, he leant his head back on the pillow again.

'That's probably enough exercise for today,' the nurse said. 'It only takes a few days of lying in bed for your muscles to become deconditioned.'

37

Meg stepped into the hospital lift. She didn't see Greg behind the bouquet of native flowers.

'Margaret?'

Meg peered through the mass of gumleaves and crimson waratahs.

'We've met a couple of times. I'm Anne's husband.'

'Greg! Of course.'

Greg lowered the bouquet. 'Is everything okay?'

Meg remembered that she was in a hospital. At her age, being in a hospital was rarely a good thing. 'Just visiting a friend. And you?'

'The safe arrival of my third grandson. Noah. Eight pounds, three ounces.'

'Congratulations.' Meg remembered the proud way Anne had held her iPad when she showed them photos of her grandchildren. She had missed the birth of Noah by less than two months.

The lift arrived at Meg's floor. She was about to launch into a hurried goodbye when Greg stepped out with her. He seemed desperate to talk.

'And your daughter, is she well?' Meg asked.

'Tired. It was an emergency caesarean.' He looked down at the flowers, studied a protea. 'At times like this she misses her mother.'

'Of course.' Meg took in Greg's crestfallen face and felt compelled to add, 'But she has you. That's something.'

Greg shook his head. 'I'm hopeless with these things. Every time she says the word *breastfeeding* I'm seized with embarrassment and terror.'

Meg's thoughts turned to Anne, of what she might have been like as a mother. She would have taken control, been the expert on everything. 'It's a lovely bouquet,' she said.

Greg beamed. 'Pippa likes things native and organic and sustainable. Even this red ribbon is biodegradable.'

The lift door opened again and they said their goodbyes— an awkward peck on the cheek above spiky flowers.

The woman at reception in the ICU told Meg that Andy had been moved to a medical ward. 'It's a good thing,' she said, and smiled.

The ward was in a new part of the hospital. It had wide hallways and white walls. The door was closed when Meg arrived. Through a narrow window she spied a shadow at the end of the bed. Curious, she knocked and entered.

Andy was only slightly less white than the starched sheets on his bed. His eyes lit up at the sight of her.

'Ming,' Andy said with a croaky voice, pointing to a slim Asian boy beside the door. 'This is Mrs Hughes, the lady I live with.'

Meg smiled in the boy's direction. 'We spoke on the phone.'

'Yes.' Ming was holding a box of chocolates. He turned back to Andy. 'Mrs Hughes told me the name of the hospital.'

They made small talk for a few uncomfortable minutes before Ming excused himself. 'I have to pack. The last exam was today and I'm flying to Hong Kong tomorrow.' He put the box of chocolates on the bedside table. 'But it was good to see you, man.' He patted Andy on the shoulder.

When Ming was gone Meg found a chair and sat down near the head of the bed.

'In Hong Kong you pay a fortune for a room like this in a private hospital,' Andy said. 'When my grandfather died, he was surrounded by five other patients.'

'How awful for him.'

'I felt sorry for the others, actually, watching him choke on his saliva, and my mum wailing and banging her head against the floor.' His voice was a whisper now. Spittle collected on his lips.

'You should rest.'

'They said the tube caused some damage to my throat.'

'Can I get you some water?'

Andy nodded.

Meg poured him a cup from the plastic jug next to the bed. He drank clumsily.

'I'm sorry,' he said when he was finished. Without his glasses he appeared younger—even more childlike and vulnerable than before.

Meg reached out and touched the bed, her fingers close to but not quite touching his arm. 'I should have put those pills away.'

Andy studied his hands. 'My aunt's on her way from Geelong. My dad's flying to Melbourne from Hong Kong.'

'Perhaps that's a good thing?' she suggested.

Andy shook his head. 'I don't know what to say to them. When my dad calls, I don't answer, I let it ring through to voicemail.'

Meg saw that she and Andy were made of the same stuff— always wanting to please, to stay quiet, to preserve the status quo.

'Atticus came back,' she said, keen to steer the conversation to happier things.

Something like a smile hovered briefly on Andy's lips. 'I know.'

'I wonder what he did while he was away.' Meg turned to the window. They were on the third floor, and she could just see the silver crown of a gum tree. 'He can speak, but he can't tell us what he wants, or what he's thinking. He copies us and we laugh. Sometimes I wonder if he's taking the mickey.'

'A mockingbird,' Andy said, before being interrupted by a knock on the door. It opened to reveal a middle-aged man with a messy hair leading a troop of young doctors.

'Andy Chan?'

'Yes?'

'We'd like to have a word with you.'

Andy, whose eyelids had been sagging, forced himself to wake up. The man with messy hair eyed Meg expectantly. She picked up her purse.

Andy shook his head. 'It's okay. Mrs Hughes can stay.'

The man gestured to one of the female doctors.

When the young woman spoke her voice was high and broken. 'The CT scan of your chest revealed some unexpected changes. We think you have a condition called extrinsic allergic alveolitis.'

Meg started at the ominous name. Rightly or wrongly, she'd always believed that the longer the name of a disease, the more serious it was. Andy's face was blank.

Another junior doctor jumped in. 'We were wondering if you've been exposed to any dust or birds recently.' The baby-faced resident turned to the man with messy hair for approval, but the consultant was studying something on his phone.

'Atticus,' Andy mumbled.

'Wait. What? You mean to say my parrot is making Andy sick?' Meg had heard of pigeon handlers getting pneumonia, but she'd always assumed it was a pigeon thing.

'Exactly.' The junior doctor sounded particularly pleased with himself. 'Andy is allergic to your pet bird.'

Meg looked at Andy, but he refused to return her gaze. She turned her attention back to the doctors. They seemed to be waiting for something, a reaction—praise, perhaps, for clinching the diagnosis. Only the female resident looked at them with anything resembling compassion.

'They call it bird fancier's lung,' the junior doctor said, when no acknowledgement of his cleverness was forthcoming. 'Maybe you've heard of it?'

Andy shook his head.

Meg couldn't believe it. A bird fancier? Andy could hardly bear to be in the same room as Atticus. The consultant rattled off the list of symptoms: cough, fever, breathlessness, loss of appetite, loss of weight, fatigue. Meg couldn't attest to the fevers, but Andy had never been a big eater, and lately she'd heard him coughing and spluttering in the early hours of the morning. Perhaps he didn't hate her spaghetti bolognese after all.

The doctors took turns listening with their stethoscopes to Andy's chest. When Andy sat forwards, his naked back showed through the gaps in his robe and Meg averted her eyes.

'Now it's my turn to say sorry,' she said when the doctors had left.

Andy made a tutting noise with his tongue. 'It's not because of Atticus that I ended up in hospital.'

'You never know. Maybe it's because of this sickness that you weren't able to concentrate on your studies.'

Though this was the explanation Andy planned on giving the university—he'd written almost the entire letter in his head by the time the doctors had finished explaining the diagnosis— he knew it wasn't true. 'I was close to failing last semester when I was living on my own—far away from you and Atticus.'

'Well, it can't have helped,' Meg insisted.

Andy pressed a red button on a remote, which loudly and slowly lowered the head of the bed.

'You must be tired,' Meg said. She picked up her handbag. The doctors hadn't said anything about Andy's discharge or his future housing arrangements, but she understood now that any hope of a cure hinged on him staying away from Atticus. If there had been any doubt before, there could be none now—Andy would have to move out.

38

Pam, the homeshare coordinator, arrived twelve minutes early. Meg had just finished tidying up and was putting on her lipstick when the doorbell rang.

'Would you like a cup of tea?' she asked as she escorted her visitor down the hallway to the kitchen.

Pam dabbed her forehead with a tissue. 'I could do with a glass of water.'

Meg pulled out a chair and Pam sat down. As she retrieved a glass from the cupboard and poured ice-water from the fridge, Meg felt the woman's eyes roaming around the room.

'How long have you lived here?' Pam asked.

'All my life.'

Pam took a notebook from her satchel and opened it on the

table. She used the palm of her hand to break the spine and flatten the pages. She scribbled a short note inside it. 'I'll need you to take me to the place where the incident happened.'

Meg placed a coaster printed with native flowers on the table and put the glass on top of it. Some water spilt onto the table. 'I'm sorry,' she said.

'I'm sure you understand how important it is for us to minimise the chance of this type of thing ever happening again.'

Meg lowered herself into the chair opposite Pam. 'I understand.'

The woman took a sip of her water before standing up. 'Shall we?'

Meg felt like a criminal directing a detective to a body. Earlier that morning she'd got down on her hands and knees to scrub the floor and the toilet. She'd even put a small plate of potpourri next to the soap dish. But her efforts went unnoticed by the inspector, who was focused solely on the cabinet above the basin.

'And is this where the offending medication was kept?'

'If you mean my sleeping tablets, then yes.'

Using her phone, Pam took a photo of the cabinet. 'The pills responsible for the near-fatal overdose.'

Meg felt her head spin. She sat down on the closed lid of the toilet.

'Are you okay?' Pam asked, her face cold.

Meg nodded. She was afraid to open her mouth for fear of what might come out.

'Perhaps I sounded a little harsh before,' Pam said. 'I didn't mean to. It's just that we take great pride in our reputation for positive outcomes. When a result falls short of our high standard, we work hard to understand why.'

'I thought he was dead when I first found him,' Meg said, and Pam winced at the word *dead*. 'He was crumpled here, in this gap between the toilet and the bath.'

'But he was okay.'

'Years ago I found my mother's body. The doctors had warned me that she might die that night, so it wasn't completely unexpected.' Meg saw Pam snatch a look at her watch, but she didn't care—she would make her listen. 'You know how sometimes you see a mannequin that looks so alive you think it might move at any minute? That's how it was for those first few hours with her body here in the house. I kept expecting her to sit up and wave her arms and laugh. I'm not a religious person. Too many bad things have happened to too many good people for me to believe in a god. But the longer I looked at my mother's dead body, the more I remembered how full of life she'd been, and the harder it was to accept that she'd just been switched off, like a light bulb. I found myself believing that something had left her body that night—some kind of invisible bubble or ball of energy that was the essence of my mother.'

Pam's lips tightened. Meg estimated her to be in her early fifties. Surely she couldn't have got this far in life without losing someone close to her.

'Luckily, on this occasion, there was no fatality,' Pam said, and opened the cabinet. She peered inside and picked up a bottle of blue nail polish remover. 'But if you're going to have another companion in future, we'll have to make some changes. You are planning on taking another companion, aren't you?'

But Meg didn't reply. She was remembering the quiet ceremony they'd had for her mother in the backyard. A handful of close friends and relatives drinking wine and listening to Judy Garland's 'Over the Rainbow' as they took turns to scatter her ashes beneath the jacaranda.

39

Life was easy at the hospital. The food was awful, but it was still better than what Mrs Hughes served up at home. Andy enjoyed the jelly, too—his parents had never let him have jelly as a child. He didn't study. The doctors had told him to rest, and he knew that a trip to the ICU would be enough to get him special consideration. The ward provided free wi-fi and he streamed Cantonese shows on his laptop. The medication appeared to be working—everything seemed less cloudy. For the first time in months he felt ready to confront the future.

Kiko arrived on Friday. Andy had been in hospital for four days. He was so engrossed in one of his shows he didn't even hear the door open. She glided in silently, like a phantom. At first, with her black hair and petite figure, Andy mistook her for the Filipina nurse who did the afternoon shift. When he saw Kiko's big brown eyes above the bouquet of daffodils his heart soared.

'Ming told me you were sick,' she explained before he could say anything.

Andy took off his glasses and cleaned them with the edge of the sheet. Kiko sat down on the chair beside the bed and laid the bouquet neatly across her legs.

'Nobody's ever bought me flowers before,' Andy said.

Kiko frowned.

'It's nice,' Andy said, but the frown remained.

Kiko pulled softly at the yellow petals of the flowers. She didn't ask Andy how he was or what was wrong with him. She spoke nervously but with purpose, as if there was something she needed to get off her chest. 'Ming wasn't sure of the exact day you were admitted.'

'It was the day of the microbiology exam,' Andy said.

Kiko pulled her water bottle from her bag and took a sip. 'I was thinking,' she said, her voice breaking, 'did you make it to the pho place?'

Weak as he still felt, Andy sensed that the power had shifted in his favour. He was surprised and a little ashamed at the joy he derived from watching Kiko squirm. If only she knew what had really happened, he thought—how bad she would feel then. He opened his mouth to reply, but Kiko didn't wait.

'The whole way here on the tram I tried to come up with an excuse,' she said. 'A car accident, gastro, a family emergency.'

Watching her lovely face contort as she spoke, Andy felt

something turn sour inside him. All of a sudden everything about her seemed forced and artificial—the pout of her lips, the lushness of her eyelashes, her childlike voice.

'But then I decided you deserved the truth.' Her mouth trembled, but her eyes were dry. 'I just don't need a boyfriend in my life right now.'

Andy didn't remember ever asking to be Kiko's boyfriend. 'It was just some beef noodle soup,' he said.

Kiko stared at Andy, her mouth no longer trembling, her thick lips pressed into an unwavering line.

He acquiesced. 'Don't worry about it.'

Kiko relaxed. Her frown disappeared. This was what she had been searching for—absolution. 'When do you get out of here?' she said, chirpy now.

Andy shrugged. 'When I'm feeling better.'

'I hope you feel better soon.'

She stayed for five minutes, making small talk about the exams and her upcoming trip to Japan, before leaving him alone with his bouquet of yellow flowers.

40

When Meg woke up the next morning, there was a puddle of blood between her legs. The shock of seeing the stain on her sheets was so great, she had to lie in bed for ten minutes before getting up to strip the mattress. She threw the bedding into the washing machine with a few spoonfuls of Vanish washing powder. She couldn't face scrubbing it by hand—watching the slow fade of the blood from the cream-coloured cotton. She remembered that Jillian had had two miscarriages before finally giving birth to her daughter. She wondered if she too had woken up, terrified, in a pool of her own blood.

Meg didn't feel hungry, but—remembering the ICU nurse's advice—she defrosted some sausages she found in the freezer. It might just have been her imagination, but she even felt a little better after eating them. She was still trying to take in what the doctor had said about Atticus causing the disease in Andy's lungs. *Alveolitis*. It was too beautiful a word to describe a life-threatening illness. It sounded like the name of an exotic flower or an expensive anti-ageing skin cream.

As she ate, Meg watched Atticus. He was perched on the windowsill next to the sink, scratching himself with his beak. She couldn't bring herself to lock the cage anymore—he was free to wander about the house as he pleased. He'd been quiet since Andy had been admitted, only occasionally singing 'Humpty Dumpty'.

When Helen had died, Atticus had been a great source of comfort to Meg. He'd been close to Helen from the start—always eager to impress her with his repertoire of nursery rhymes. After she died, it was as if Helen had lived on in the parrot and his poetry. Now, in the wake of Andy's illness, Meg saw Atticus in a different light. She couldn't forget the way he'd jumped around the bathroom while the paramedics were working on Andy—competing for their attention, distracting them from their task. She was reminded of an Emily Dickinson poem she'd studied during high school:

A bird came down the walk:
He did not know I saw;
He bit an angle-worm in halves
And ate the fellow, raw.

And then, he drank a dew
From a convenient grass,

And then hopped sidewise to the wall
To let a beetle pass.

She'd written an essay about how the poem demonstrated the efficient and practical nature of animals—how they took what they needed without remorse, but how they never took more than they needed. Meg recalled that she'd got a very good mark for that essay, but she also remembered that, even as she wrote it, she could think of numerous examples that contradicted Dickinson's position—the neighbour's cat, who killed a mouse after hours of tormenting it; the ducks at the creek who ate more than their fill of bread before chasing the other ducks away. In Meg's opinion animals were more like humans than humans gave them credit for. Atticus, who knew nothing of the wild or how to survive it, had flown away from her the first chance he got. Maybe Helen, too, would've escaped, if given the opportunity.

The washing machine beeped to let her know the cycle had finished. As she hung her wet sheets on the line, the doorbell rang. She wondered if it was Pam, returning to cast her forensic eye over the place again. Meg took her time, clipping the last peg over the sheet before going in to answer the door.

'Jill,' she said, surprised.

'Well, you certainly took your time. I was about to call the police.'

Meg couldn't tell if she was joking.

'I brought coffee,' Jillian said, and held up a cardboard tray containing two takeaway cups. 'And cake.'

Meg opened the screen door. Jillian followed her down the hall to the lounge room. As Meg turned on the light, she suppressed her shock at all the dust and cobwebs. She'd been so preoccupied with Patrick, and Andy, she hadn't cleaned in weeks. Even the windows, expertly polished by Andy not long ago, had regained their earlier cloudiness. But she would not apologise to Jillian. She sat stiffly in one of the armchairs.

Jillian tried her best to arrange herself elegantly on the lounge, but the laxity of the springs and the softness of the cushions made it difficult. Meg sat back and enjoyed watching her friend disappear into the couch.

'Greg told me he saw you at the hospital. Visiting a friend,' Jillian said, once she'd found a comfortable position.

'Yes.' Meg knew what Jillian was thinking: *But you don't have any friends, except me.*

'Did something happen to the Chinese boy?'

'His name's Andy. And he's not a boy.'

'I knew it.'

Meg leant forwards and picked up one of the takeaway cups Jillian had set down on the coffee table. 'Why are you here, Jillian?' she said. 'To say sorry? Because this doesn't feel much like an apology.'

Perhaps it was the surprise of seeing Meg so assertive, or perhaps it was just tiredness—whatever the cause, Jillian surrendered.

'I'm sorry,' she said. It was the first time in their seventy years of friendship that Jillian had apologised to Meg. 'Something happened to me when Anne died. It was so abrupt, so unexpected. It rattled me to my core. And then a few weeks later the doctor called to say they'd found an abnormality on my mammogram. It was nothing in the end, but it was bloody terrifying.'

Meg felt her hands move to her lower abdomen, as if to shield Jillian from the sight of her bleeding uterus. Tears stabbed her eyes. Meg couldn't remember ever seeing Jillian as honest and vulnerable as this, and she didn't quite know how to deal with it. On the one hand it was reassuring to know that someone as strong as Jillian shared her fears, but on the other hand it was frightening to realise that the rock she'd clung to for so long was itself brittle.

'I'm sorry too,' Meg said, hating herself just a little. Sometimes she felt as if she'd spent half her life apologising, when most of the time she'd done nothing wrong. But today, watching her once-formidable friend look small and lost on the couch, she was sorry. Sorry they were getting old. Sorry they were scared. Sorry death seemed to be waiting for them around every corner.

Jillian stood up, instantly resuming her invincible air. She sat on the edge of Meg's armchair and draped her long arm around Meg's shoulder. At her friend's touch, Meg dissolved. The words and the tears came hot and fast. She told Jillian everything. She told her about finding Andy wedged between the toilet and the bath. She told her about Atticus's dramatic escape and quiet return. She told her about her dirty getaway with Patrick that she'd called off before it had even begun. She told her about how she was slowly haemorrhaging from her unused womb. With each confession, Meg felt Jillian grow stronger beside her. She watched her friend's spine become straighter, her neck longer, her shoulders squarer. It was just what they needed. A restoration of order.

41

There was something reassuring and predictable about hospital life. Andy felt like a little cog in a clunky but reliable machine. Every morning at six-thirty, a nurse measured his blood pressure. An hour later, breakfast was delivered by a round woman with a brassy laugh. Sometime between eight and nine o'clock, the doctors did their ward round. Every day a nurse checked to make sure Andy had passed urine and opened his bowels. Every day a doctor examined Andy for early signs of malfunction. Rather than degrading or infantilising, the attention was liberating for Andy. He was free from worry because there were lots of other people—professional people—doing the worrying for him.

He knew it couldn't last forever, but he was caught off

guard when the doctors told him he was about to be discharged. The news created a stir of panic. Where would he go? He couldn't go back to living with Mrs Hughes and Atticus. Ming was an option, but they'd had those harsh words only the week before. His aunt had called a couple of times, but she lived all the way out in Geelong and had children of her own. Winnie said his father was on his way, but Andy didn't know where he planned to stay, especially after spending so much money on an air ticket. The last thing Andy wanted to do was dig his dad even deeper into debt. His health insurance was paying for his hospital stay, and so long as he remained an inpatient, he could hide behind his illness.

Andy thought back to his discussion with the psychiatry registrar the day before. He'd been truthful with her, denying any thoughts of suicide when she'd asked him, but if he'd known they were planning to release him five days after his near-fatal overdose, he would've lied freely and excessively.

There was something else too. Andy enjoyed being cared for. As long as he could remember, his father had worked long hours, and his mother, when she was home, was always busy, chopping vegetables for dinner and finding some new surface that needed cleaning. Most of Andy's childhood, when he wasn't at school, had been spent in his room, playing computer games and assembling model aeroplanes. Andy had been glad of the company of his yeh yeh, who'd grown gentle with his advancing dementia. Thinking of his grandfather now had a calming effect on Andy. He closed his eyes and remembered the topography of the old man's hands—the mushroom-coloured spots, the meandering veins, the bowed and knotted tendons.

Andy was roused minutes later by a loud knock at the door to his room. Through the blue screen he saw the silhouette of a small woman with gigantic hair.

'Auntie!' he said as a brightly made-up face peeked from behind the curtain.

'Fresh chicken congee,' Winnie said by way of a hello and placed a large Tupperware bowl on the tray in front of him. 'Better than any medicine.'

Andy put his hand on the bowl. It was still warm.

'I put it in an esky in the boot with lots of bubble wrap to keep it hot and stop it from spilling.'

'Very clever.'

His aunt looked him up and down. 'You're so pale,' she said, and pinched his cheek, hard, in an attempt to inject some colour.

Andy wondered how much the staff at the hospital had told her over the phone while he was unconscious.

'I should have come to Melbourne more often,' she said. 'But it's such a long drive with all the traffic, and with all the kids' after-school activities, it's hard to find the time. Who would've thought that after all those years of studying commerce I'd end up an unpaid chauffeur.'

Andy took this to be an apology. He thought back to the day of the exam, when he'd seen his aunt drinking and laughing at the café. 'That's okay,' he said.

'And what a stupid idea, getting you to live with an old woman. You're not a carer. You're a child. You need someone to look after you.'

'It wasn't Mrs Hughes' fault—it was her pet parrot.

I developed an allergy to it.' As he spoke, Andy realised how ridiculous the words sounded.

Winnie stared at him with her black eyes. 'You know, when I first came to Australia with Uncle Craig, I found it hard too. That was twenty years ago, and we were living in Geelong. Can you imagine? From Hong Kong to Geelong! It wasn't even Melbourne. Everybody went surfing and camping on the weekends, and I'd never even sat on grass before.'

Andy looked down at his toes, poking out from beneath the bedsheets.

'I was lonely,' Winnie said. 'But I didn't give up.'

'It was an allergy,' Andy said again.

'Now look at me!' his aunt went on. 'My pavlova was voted the best dessert at my daughter's school fete last year. I barrack for the Cats. I can even stand up for a good five seconds on a surfboard.'

'Are you happy?' Andy said.

Winnie paused. 'Of course I miss things about Hong Kong. The food. The efficiency. The way you can buy something without talking to somebody about how your day was— I mean, how good can my day possibly be if I'm spending it in a supermarket buying yoghurt and tampons?'

Andy laughed.

'But thoughts like that will poison your insides.' She shuddered, as though shaking off any lingering nostalgia. 'Best to try new things.'

So his aunt knew everything.

'What did Dad say?'

'I called him the day the hospital notified me. He said he'd

202

get on the next plane to Melbourne, but it's taken him a while to get the money together and flights are always crowded this time of year. I would have come up earlier too, but I had a bit of a crisis of my own. It's all sorted now, though, thankfully.'

Andy thought of his father—his greying hair, and the stooped way he walked, as if he bore the weight of the universe on his shoulders.

'I didn't tell him everything, of course,' Winnie added, reading Andy's mind. 'Your mother gives him enough stress.'

Andy's mother hated Winnie. When he was a boy, she used to say his aunt had the voice of a crow, the head of an ox and the tongue of a cobra.

'Where is he?'

'His plane arrives tonight. I'll stay with him in a hotel in the city. We'll pick you up first thing tomorrow morning.'

Andy couldn't tell if he felt relieved or anxious. He was happy he had somewhere to go and overcome with a strong desire to see his father. But he was worried. He wasn't sure he could bear to see the disappointment on his dad's face. The last thing Andy wanted was to make his father hang his head any lower.

42

Meg hadn't been to a doctor in years. When her knees had first played up she'd spent a lot of time at the surgery down the road, where the doctors had given her painkillers that made her nauseated and drowsy. They'd insisted on doing lots of other tests too—things completely unrelated to her arthritis. She'd eventually grown tired of walking out of the consulting room with a list of tasks—*lose weight, eat better, join a gym, try pilates*—or referrals for investigations that came with their own set of instructions—*don't eat anything for ten hours, call this number, do a poo into an old ice-cream container.*

It had been so long, in fact, that she didn't recognise any of the doctors' photos pinned to the corkboard. But the waiting room—in spite of its new carpet and fresh coat of paint—still prompted memories of Helen shuddering with a forty-degree fever.

Meg was glad that Jill had insisted on accompanying her. She didn't want her friend inside the consultation room, but it was reassuring to know she'd be just outside the door, ready and waiting to put her back together again. As Jillian flicked through a tattered magazine, Meg practised in her head what she would say to the doctor. *It's rather embarrassing. I should have come earlier. I'm afraid I might be bleeding to death.*

The doctor was a man in his fifties with a sad face and a tired voice. She followed him down the corridor to the consulting room. He was already seated at his desk by the time she walked through the door.

'How can I help?' he asked in the bored tone of a super-market cashier.

Meg looked at the doctor's desk. There was an empty coffee mug that read *Sometimes the best thing about my job is that the chair spins.* Next to the mug was a messy pile of papers. On the wall above the desk there was a framed medical degree. The words *Bachelor of Medicine* and *Bachelor of Surgery* were just visible through a furry layer of dust on the glass.

'I'm bleeding. From down below. I don't think that's supposed to happen at my age.'

He took her blood pressure with a machine, taking care not to let his fingers touch her skin. He printed a referral form for an ultrasound.

'We should probably do a pap test,' he said, looking at the computer screen. 'But I'm sure you'd prefer a female doctor.'

Meg didn't care about the sex of her doctor, but she did

prefer one who didn't seem completely repulsed by the idea of examining her.

'Go to the girls at reception. They'll make you an appointment with one of my colleagues.'

When Meg returned to the waiting room, Jillian stood up and scanned her face. Meg smiled a tight-lipped smile and Jillian breathed a sigh of relief. The entire consultation must have taken less than ten minutes, and in a way Meg was grateful. She'd been anticipating a painful, teary breakdown. She knew that with the right GP—someone who leant in and looked at her with caring eyes—she would have dissolved into a blithering mess. But with the sad, tired doctor such displays of emotion would have been impossible.

They said nothing as they walked to the car. It was only when they'd stopped at the first set of lights that Meg mentioned the ultrasound.

'Of course I'll take you,' Jillian said, even though Meg hadn't asked her to.

In all their years of friendship, Meg had never thought of Jillian as a caring person. She'd listened to her moan about flying to Sydney to rescue her daughter from yet another failed relationship, and she'd heard her complain about paying the night nurse to care for her dying mother. Jillian could perform when she needed to—like she had that day at Anne's memorial—but Meg knew that, deep down, her friend was pragmatic and unsentimental. In a way she still was—there were no tears, no hands on arms or reassuring words—but there was a thoughtfulness to her behaviour

206

that was both moving and unexpected.

'I got the call from BreastScreen on a Friday,' Jillian said as they rounded the bend towards Meg's house. 'I spent the whole weekend not knowing if I had cancer. I stood for hours in front of the mirror staring at my left breast and trying to figure it out.'

Meg's hands migrated again to the fleshy spot above her pubic bone.

Jillian flicked her sunglasses down from her head to cover her eyes. 'My sister-in-law who had a similar experience last year said the not knowing was the hardest thing. She said that once she knew, she could just get on and deal with it. But I think that's bullshit. I'm pretty sure finding out you have cancer is worse than not knowing if you do.'

Whatever comfort Meg had taken from the doctor's matter-of-fact manner was quickly dissipating. 'What are you saying?'

Jillian parked the car in front of Meg's home and pulled up the handbrake. She looked through the windscreen at the old house and mumbled, 'I don't know.'

43

Andy could feel his heart beat faster as the morning wore on. He hadn't seen his parents in nine months. Even though Andy knew his aunt had shielded his father from the worst of the news, Andy was anxious about their impending meeting. As sick as he was, he'd still failed his exams, and his father was still paying the exorbitant university fees. Up until now, Andy had only seen things from his own point of view—the pressure to perform, the lack of affection, the fact that he'd had to give up his flat and move in with a stranger because his parents could no longer cover his rent. As he packed his things into a plastic bag—the T-shirt and jeans he'd been wearing the day he collapsed, the chocolates from Ming and the toiletry bag Mrs Hughes had kindly brought from home—he imagined the dismay his father must have felt when Winnie called to give him the news.

Afterwards, he sat on the edge of his bed and waited. It was a hot, clear November day. The only clouds were white wisps, like strands of fairy floss drifting across the sky. Though Melbourne had a reputation for terrible weather, Andy knew his lasting memories of Australia would be of that big blue dome of sky. He was still staring out the window when Winnie and his father arrived.

'Here he is!' his aunt announced loudly in Cantonese.

Andy turned around to see his father, small and embarrassed, hiding behind Winnie's bouffant hair and bright lipstick.

His father stepped forward and placed a cool hand on Andy's shoulder. 'Your mother wanted to be here, but the doctors said she shouldn't travel.'

Andy looked at the floor. He wasn't ready to see what emotions were bubbling behind his father's eyes.

'Is this it?' Winnie asked, picking up the plastic bag with a disgusted look.

Andy nodded. 'I'll have to collect the rest of my stuff from Rose Street.'

'The house where you lived with the old lady and her bird?' his father asked.

Andy flinched. His father was not an animal person. He often recoiled in horror if a pigeon perched on the windowsill of their apartment.

'It's not the parrot's fault,' Andy said, and watched his father shake his head.

At that moment, a junior doctor came in brandishing an envelope with Andy's discharge documents. Andy grabbed it and buried it in his pocket before his father could ask to see it. There was probably nothing to worry about—his father couldn't read English and his aunt wouldn't translate it truthfully for him—but he still felt better when the paperwork was safely out of sight. After the doctor left, the pharmacist arrived with prednisolone tablets and a steroid inhaler. He checked Andy's technique and reminded him to rinse his mouth with water after using the puffer. Andy's aunt and father watched on silently—Winnie grinning, his father frowning.

Once the nurse said Andy was free to go, they climbed into Winnie's four-wheel drive in the hospital car park. Next to his aunt, who was barely five foot tall, the mud-splattered car looked the size of a tank. Andy was surprised she could reach the pedals. But she drove it expertly, and fast, handling the machine as if it was a bulky extension of her body. Once or twice Andy saw his dad grip the armrest so hard his knuckles blanched bony white.

'Do you still have your key?' his aunt asked as she weaved between vehicles.

'Yes, but I should probably let her know we're coming.' Andy pulled his phone from his pocket. He hoped Mrs Hughes wouldn't answer, that he could just leave a message—anything was better than having an audience for their conversation— but she picked up on the second ring.

'Andy!' She sounded pleased to hear from him.

'They discharged me.'

'That's wonderful news.'

Andy could hear Atticus whistling 'Auld Lang Syne' in the background. 'I'll need to pick up my things,' he said.

'Of course.'

'Make sure she removes the bird from the house before we get there!' his aunt shouted, loudly enough for Mrs Hughes to hear.

'Would it be okay,' Andy said, glaring at his aunt in the rear-view mirror, 'if you put Atticus outside? For five minutes while I pack?'

'Of course.'

Andy wanted to give her some kind of warning, a pre-emptive apology for his family, but it was impossible. 'We're on our way from the hospital.'

'I'll see you soon.'

'Bye.'

'I should never have suggested you move in with that filthy old woman,' Winnie said when Andy had hung up the phone. Andy knew this was his aunt's way of apologising to his father. He could tell from his dad's folded arms and tight lips that he hadn't forgiven her.

When they pulled up in front of the house, Winnie opened the glove box and three crumpled face masks fell to the floor.

'One for each of us,' she said.

Andy felt a rising nausea. It was as if two worlds were colliding at great speed and he could do nothing to stop them.

As they walked up the short gravel path to the house, Andy's father bent his head to avoid an overhanging tree branch. The garden was even more overgrown than when

Andy had first moved in—the weeds more unruly, the boundary between house and yard less defined. Andy didn't need to see his father's face to know what he was thinking. It was the same repulsion he'd felt on arriving at Rose Street a few months ago. Except now that feeling had been replaced by something quite different—a defensiveness and protectiveness that Andy wasn't used to. He supposed somewhere along the way he'd become fond of the house on Rose Street.

Winnie made way for Andy, who inserted his key into the lock. His mask hung loose around his neck—he couldn't bear to put it on. When Winnie pulled it above his nose he felt as if he was suffocating.

As the latch gave way, Andy stepped inside. Winnie and his father followed close behind him. It was a hot day, but the old house felt cool. Andy saw the bright kitchen beaming at the end of the corridor.

'Andy?'

The sun rendered Mrs Hughes a silhouette in the hallway. Her white hair formed a nimbus around her head. As she shuffled closer, Andy saw that she looked washed out, like a jumper that had lost its colour after years of wear.

'You must be Andy's parents,' she said, ignoring the face masks.

Winnie pushed her way to the front. 'I'm his aunt, and this is his father.' She spoke in a curt tone unlike any Andy had heard her use before.

'Can I get you a cold drink?' Mrs Hughes asked. 'It's a scorcher today.'

'No thank you,' Winnie replied for all of them. 'We're on

our way to Geelong. We're only here for a few minutes.'

Mrs Hughes' pale eyes scanned the three masked faces in front of her. Andy wondered what the old lady was thinking. It was hard to tell from her cheery performance. He hoped she saw in his eyes some of the sorrow he was feeling.

'Take your time,' she said, and walked back towards the sunny kitchen.

44

The radiology centre was located inside a private hospital. Jillian was waiting for Meg in the hospital café. Meg put on the baby-blue gown the sonographer had given her. Like most hospital gowns, it was open at the back. Meg held the two loose edges together with her hand. She followed the sonographer down the dark corridor, her feet padding across the tiles. At the end of the hall they reached a consulting room, unlit except by the ghostly screen of a monitor. Meg lay down on the bed as she was told. Her eyes scanned the giant tubes of lubricant and the long ultrasound probe in its sheath.

As the sonographer fiddled with the computer, Meg tried to recall another time she'd felt as vulnerable as this—lying on a paper sheet with her legs spread, waiting to find out if she had cancer. The only thing that came even vaguely close was the hour she'd spent in the emergency department immediately after Helen's accident. She'd been sixteen at the time, not yet an adult, but she was learning to trust her gut instinct. Her gut instinct that day had told her that Helen would never walk again, and her gut instinct today told her that she had a dirty big tumour in her pelvis.

The sonographer began with some images of her abdomen. She rolled the probe across Meg's belly, diving deep into a fleshy valley before gliding gently across dimpled skin. She took a few quick photos before changing probes and directing Meg to the toilet to empty her bladder.

'In postmenopausal women this next bit can be pretty uncomfortable,' the sonographer said when Meg was lying on the bed again. 'But we use a generous amount of lubricant to try and minimise the discomfort.' To demonstrate, the sonographer squeezed the tube of gel enthusiastically. It made a loud farting noise, and for a moment Meg considered making a joke of it—that's what Helen would have done— but the sonographer said nothing, and so Meg, too, pretended it hadn't happened.

Instead she focused on the computer monitor. She watched the white haze form vague and beautiful shapes, like cumulus clouds, across the black screen. Every so often the probe— which the sonographer referred to as a wand—hovered mid-arc, and a tiny cursor appeared. When this happened the sonographer would type something: *R ovary* or *uterus*. Other times there was a dotted line between two crosses, and a measurement in millimetres flashed across the screen.

Lastly an orb of white materialised, glowing like a full moon. The sonographer spent a long time measuring it from various angles. Eventually she froze the picture and went to fetch the doctor, leaving Meg on the bed in the dark, with nothing to look at except the globe, gleaming like a giant Christmas bauble on the monitor.

The doctor introduced himself as Dr McDougall before unfreezing the picture and picking up the wand. He frowned at the screen.

'Have you been bleeding?'

'Yes.' Meg gripped the paper sheet beneath her, which disintegrated into ragged pieces between her fingers. She didn't dare ask him what the white ball was, preferring to lie quietly on the bed as cold gel oozed out of her. The doctor took some more measurements and ordered Meg to see her GP ASAP, which he pronounced *A-sap,* as if it was a word and not an acronym.

When the doctor had gone, the sonographer gave Meg a box of tissues to wipe herself and then escorted her back to the cubicle. Meg got dressed slowly, her eyes blinded by the changing-room lights after so long in the darkness. Everywhere she looked she could see a black mark in the shape of a ball—as if, instead of an image of her womb, she had looked directly at the sun.

In the hospital café, Jillian was so busy typing on her phone she didn't see Meg arrive. Meg thought back to her first day of school, scanning the faces of her new class for someone strong to attach herself to—someone who wasn't chewing their fingernails or sucking their thumb. She had quickly settled on Jillian—a tall girl sitting straight-backed at a desk in the front row, her dark hair pulled into tight pigtails. When Jillian had noticed Meg staring, she'd waved and pointed to the empty desk beside her. Perhaps even then she'd spotted something that needed fixing in that timid little girl.

Now, when Meg tapped her on the shoulder, Jillian looked up with worried eyes. 'So?'

'They didn't say anything.'

Jillian seemed dismayed, and Meg felt the need to reassure her.

'Not that I'd know, but it looked okay to me.'

Jillian smiled and Meg saw a flash of the grin that had greeted her from the front of the classroom all those years ago. The teeth were bigger and yellower and some weren't even real, but the smile was the same, which made Meg happy and sad and nostalgic all at once. She supposed this was how it was when you were dying—the tiniest and most trivial things became weighty with history.

Jillian paid for her coffee and disappeared to the toilet. Meg waited for her at the entrance to the café. The café opened onto an internal foyer, which was surrounded by specialist consulting rooms—glass cages with water coolers and maroon-coloured chairs. As she scanned the rooms, something made her eyes linger on the hunched figure of an older gentleman. His elbows were on his knees and his head was bowed. She couldn't see his face. His hat had been placed on the seat beside him and a rolled-up newspaper hung, limp, from his hand.

She recognised him, finally, by the heart-shaped bald patch

on the crown of his head. Even then it was hard to believe it was the same man. He looked so defeated, so different from the Patrick she had come to know. Meg read the plaque on the glass door across from him: *Associate Professor Gordon Lam, Urologist.*

Just before Jillian returned, Meg saw Patrick stand up and approach the receptionist. He asked her a question and then laughed in his loud, exaggerated way. Almost as an afterthought he reached out and touched the back of the receptionist's hand. The woman smiled, but as Patrick walked away, Meg saw her shake her head.

Meg knew Patrick was a sexist and possibly a racist and yet here she was, choked with pity for his loneliness. It was as if some emotional dial inside her had been turned to high. Perhaps, Meg pondered, it was this—rather than the quietly growing mass in her pelvis—that would kill her in the end. She took Jillian's arm for fear that her own legs wouldn't hold her. To her relief, Jillian didn't flinch or pull away.

45

'I could sue her.'

They'd just reached Geelong. It was quiet in the car and everyone was drowsy from the hum of the engine.

'The agency maybe. Not the old lady,' said Winnie.

Andy, who'd been drifting off to sleep, sat up.

His father made a grunting noise. 'This would never have happened if she hadn't had a parrot. Why do people in Australia like living with animals? They cause disease. Everybody knows that.'

On one level Andy was pleased. He assumed his father's anger originated, at least in some part, from a place of love. But the thought of Mrs Hughes receiving a tightly worded lawyer's letter after all that awkwardness with the face masks made him sick to his stomach. Still, he said nothing. His father had dropped everything and flown seven thousand kilometres to see him. The appropriate response from a dutiful son was agreement—at worst, a quiet acquiescence. Andy hoped these threats would disappear once the shock of the diagnosis had faded. His father had always been critical of lawyers, and equally critical of people who sued for what he called *the bad luck of life*. But Andy hadn't spent a lot of time with his father in recent years. It was possible he had changed.

It was a relief to arrive at Winnie's rambling house in Geelong. As the car pulled into the driveway they were greeted by a muscular German shepherd. Andy saw his dad tense up. Winnie opened her door to have her cheek licked by a long pink tongue.

In the front yard, Christmas lights had been strung between two trees. A pair of children with bare feet and bed hair burst through the peeling front door of the house. Andy stole a glance at his father, who was looking at Winnie, perplexed. For the first time Andy noticed how out of place his father appeared in Australia—he stood out, bright and conspicuous, like an animal in an unfamiliar habitat.

Once inside, Winnie led them to their room. Andy eyed the double bed, draped in a peacock-print doona. Above the headboard, stuck to the wall, was a poster of a rainbow with the words *Jesus Loves You* in Chinese characters.

As far as Andy could remember, he'd never shared a room with his father. He felt nervous about sleeping so close to this man who was such a mystery to him. From the stiff way his father rolled his suitcase in and stowed it in the corner, Andy presumed he felt the same.

For a few awkward moments they stood at opposite sides of the room, each in the narrow trench between the bed and the wall. Andy was relieved when his dad suggested they join the others, and he breathed easier when they reached the light-filled space at the back of the house. The home was bigger than any apartment Andy had visited in Hong Kong, but somehow it seemed more cluttered, with no clear markers of where one area began and another ended. Beanbags sat, slouched, beside cardboard boxes full of fruit. A pair of dirty socks lay next to a naked Barbie doll. In front of the TV there was a paint palette holding Lego and a half-eaten chocolate doughnut. But it was cheerful, with scattered jars of fresh flowers, and the children's drawings taped to the walls. At the very rear of the house, bi-fold doors opened onto a small overgrown lawn. Beyond the lawn, near the fence, a wooden cubbyhouse hovered above four stilts and a rope ladder. The children—twins, Marcus and Maddie—hung from it, screeching like monkeys.

Winnie busied herself in the kitchen, preparing dinner. Winnie's husband, Craig, emerged from behind the door of the enormous fridge, holding three frosted bottles of beer.

'Winnie said you don't drink, but can I tempt you with a VB?'

Andy's father grabbed one of the bottles. Craig beamed and said, 'Good man.' It wasn't true that his father didn't drink— as a young boy, Andy had found an impressive collection of whisky bottles beneath his parents' bed. Andy followed his father's lead and accepted a beer. He took a sip. The bitterness made him wince and the bubbles burned his nostrils. He looked at his dad, leaning against the bi-fold doors, taking casual swigs from his bottle. There was so much he still didn't know about this man.

Andy sat down on the couch, a deep three-seater plastered with dog hair. When the twins ran screaming into the room, Craig put down his beer and tossed them one at a time into the air. Watching them, Andy felt as if he'd been transported onto the set of an American sitcom. He stole another look at his father, but if his dad felt any guilt, or deficiency, watching this scene of rough family affection, he didn't show it. If anything he seemed distracted, his eyes staring past Craig and the twins, through the lush garden to the coast and beyond.

Just then Winnie called them for dinner—a colourful buffet of homemade sushi, chicken satay, potato wedges, fried rice, and spaghetti and meatballs. Andy's stomach rumbled. He hadn't eaten since he'd left the hospital. He filled his plate as Winnie looked on approvingly. When he sat down she grabbed his cheek between her sharp fingers.

'You're so skinny,' she said. 'Like a skeleton.'

Andy's father steered clear of the spaghetti and potato wedges, which had been mauled by the sticky hands of the twins, and piled his plate high with sushi and rice. As they ate, the conversation swung, pendulum-like, between Cantonese and English. Winnie handled it all expertly, weaving Craig into the discussion just before he felt frustrated, and finding enough common ground between them to maintain an entertaining—if superficial—discussion. When she left the table to retrieve the dessert from the overflowing fridge, they sat in drunken silence. Andy listened to the beat of his pulse in his ears—a loud, panicky rhythm, eased only by the reappearance of Winnie, bearing mango puddings the colour of the sun.

Andy felt like a newly freed prisoner who, after six months of eating only gruel, was dining at a five-star restaurant. Even his father, a picky eater, had eaten every grain of rice on his plate. Andy sat back in his chair, happily full and slightly tipsy.

'Winnie, can you ask Craig what he thinks about me suing the homeshare agency?' Andy's father said coolly, as if asking for another beer.

Winnie translated the question for Craig as Andy slumped lower in his seat. Craig had done a combined arts law degree for one year at university before dropping the law component. He now worked as a freelance web designer, but he was the closest thing they had to a lawyer in the family.

'I'd have to look at the specifics, but I think you have a good case.'

Andy felt Craig's blue eyes pause on his face before they flicked back to his father. He wondered how much Winnie had told him.

'You'd probably have to prove what long-term consequences Andy has suffered as a result of the illness. And whether everything was done to minimise the risk to tenants. The greater the damage, the greater the payout.'

Winnie translated, and Andy's father promptly delivered a list: 'My son's long-term health, his academic grades, his chances of getting into medicine next year.'

With each item on the list Andy felt a sharp blow to his

chest. Perhaps his aunt saw this, because she stood up and started clearing their plates. 'Lawyers are expensive,' she said. 'You'll have to work out if it's worth it.'

Craig leant back in his chair. 'Winnie's always complaining about how I dropped my law degree.'

'If he hadn't,' Winnie said, looking at him with laughing eyes, 'we wouldn't have to live in Geelong. We'd be living in North Shore Sydney!'

Andy smiled, but he wasn't listening. All his senses were attuned to his father—studying his unreadable face for signs of a shift, a surrender, a softening of his heart.

46

They were almost back at Meg's house when Jillian pulled over next to the bottle shop. Ever since the late 1970s, there'd been a liquor store at the end of Rose Street. It was where Meg's mother had bought her sherry, and her father had bought his beer.

'For old times' sake,' Jillian said.

Meg waited in the car. The store looked unfamiliar. It was no longer owned by Giovanni with the mermaid tattoo—he'd sold it to a wine retailer decades ago and bought a house in Sicily with the money. Now it had a big neon sign out the front and was staffed by a uni student in a black T-shirt. But it still sold beer and wine—for now, that was all that mattered.

When they were teenagers, it had become something of

a ritual for Meg and Jillian to raid the liquor cabinet when Meg's parents went out. To avoid suspicion, they never took too much of anything—a few drops of sherry here, a splash of port there. Sometimes, if they were feeling really courageous, they might risk a sip from Meg's father's twenty-year-old scotch whisky. Afterwards, they would lounge on a picnic blanket in the backyard, nursing their revolting drinks and staring up at the tent of stars. Sometimes Helen would join them and sometimes she wouldn't, depending on her mood. They talked about everything and nothing—boys, music, books, how annoying their parents were, what they'd dreamt about the night before.

Jillian's eyes were electric when she emerged from the bottle shop brandishing a brown paper bag. She sped the rest of the way home. Meg found the old picnic blanket in the linen cupboard. As she laid the blanket down on the grass, her knees made a cracking sound. Meg wondered if this attempt to recapture a moment of youthful pleasure was a little pathetic. But it felt good to lie down. These days it always felt good to lie down. She looked up through the lattice of leaves.

Jillian had bought a thirty-dollar shiraz. It was a far cry from the noxious cocktails of the past, but in a nod to their adolescence, they drank it straight from the bottle.

'I saw Patrick at the hospital,' Meg said when Jillian lay down beside her.

'Oh yeah? What was he doing there?'

'Seeing a professor of urology.'

'That's prostate, isn't it?'

'I think so.' Meg shielded her eyes from a shaft of sunlight.

'Cancer, probably.'

'He never mentioned anything,' Meg said, and then remembered her bleeding.

'He can't be that unwell,' Jillian said, sitting up and taking a swig from the bottle. 'Greg said he's taken up Latin dancing.'

Meg imagined Patrick in a sleek black tango suit and heels.

'In a way, I admire him,' Jillian said. 'Putting himself out there, trying new things. I wish Henry was more like that.'

In all the years Jillian had been married, Meg had never really got to know her husband. She could count on one hand the number of times she'd visited their big house in the eastern suburbs. Jillian liked to keep things compartmentalised, and this extended to her relationships. She'd met Henry at university. Meg was from a different era.

'He really panicked during the whole breast thing. Kept talking about how he couldn't cope without me. It was like I was already dead.' She handed Meg the bottle. 'When we found out it was just a scare, he went back to normal.' She clicked her fingers. 'Just like that. Calling me to remind me to buy bananas and shaving cream from the supermarket the very next day, as if nothing had happened.'

Meg sat up and sculled from the bottle. She wiped her mouth with the back of her sleeve. 'When Helen had her accident, some friends left piles of home-cooked food on the doorstep. Others crossed the street to avoid talking to us.'

'Bastards,' Jillian said, and belched.

Meg laughed and lay back down on the long grass. 'I think they felt guilty.'

'Well, I know my brother was banned from climbing trees after that.'

It was the first time they'd spoken about the accident in sixty years.

'Mum insisted on calling a man to cut down the paperbark a week later. The night before he was due to come, I heard Dad attack the trunk with an axe. I peeked through the window, but it was pitch black—I couldn't see a thing. I just heard the terrifying noise of him hacking and grunting and weeping.'

'I remember walking to your house and hearing the siren and thinking it was for somebody else,' Jillian said, her voice strained. 'When I saw the ambulance out front I knew something terrible had happened. I followed the screams to the backyard. Hel was on the ground. Her eyes were terrified, but her legs were soft—the top one fell across the bottom one as if she was posing for a photo.'

As Jillian spoke Meg closed her eyes. She felt a breeze, gentle as a caress across her cheek. She wanted to tell Jillian that she often imagined Helen's ashes dissolving into tiny particles, being sucked up by the trunk of the jacaranda and re-emerging, reassembled and reconfigured, in the purple petals of the tree. But even now, tipsy on wine, she couldn't find the courage to articulate her silly fantasy. Instead she lay on the grass and listened to her friend's drunken sighs and the whisper of the leaves until she couldn't tell where the plant noises began and the human noises ended.

DECEMBER

47

It was the first day of the school holidays and Winnie was driving them to the beach. Andy sat squashed between the twins' car seats while his father sat up front. It was the first time Andy had been to the beach since moving to Melbourne. The twins were bubbling with excitement. They kicked and prodded Andy, and if he didn't give them the reaction they wanted, they leant across him to kick and prod each other. Andy was happy to get out of the four-wheel drive when they arrived at the breezy beach. The twins ran ahead.

'They're strong swimmers,' Winnie said, her face beaming.

Andy hadn't learnt to swim until he was a teenager. His dad had taught him one weekend at Repulse Bay beach. Now he watched his cousins run into the ocean and felt jealous of their fearlessness. They might share blood through his auntie, but these kids with their round eyes and floppy hair were Australian in a way Andy knew he never could be.

'The sun will be good for you,' his aunt said, and patted him, hard, on the back.

Andy bowed his head. Today was the first day he'd woken up feeling refreshed. It turned out sharing a room with his father wasn't so bad after all. He'd found it reassuring to hear the gentle breath of another person when he woke up, as he always did, multiple times a night. During the day his aunt and her family acted as the perfect buffer between him and his dad. For the first ten minutes he'd even enjoyed the excited holiday vibe in the car. But now his aunt's words reminded him of his illness and exposed the unease he'd managed to bury the night before. He looked at his father, who hadn't heard what Winnie had said. He was walking a few paces behind them and had paused to look up at the sky. It was only for a minute, but Andy took this moment of mindfulness to be a positive sign—surely legal battles were the furthest thing from his father's mind.

They set up their umbrellas and towels near the edge of the water. Winnie had packed an esky with honey soy chicken wings and homemade Vietnamese rice paper rolls. After she had given Andy and his father a paper plate and ordered them to eat, she joined her children in the water. Andy watched his aunt splashing and squealing and marvelled at the difference between brother and sister.

'Australia is a good place for Winnie,' his father said, as if reading Andy's mind. He didn't say Australia wasn't a good place for them, but he didn't have to—it was evident from their impractical shoes and the stiff way they sat on their beach towels.

Andy bit into a rice paper roll. It was cold and fresh and the prawn was sweet. His father did the same. With their mouths full they had no option but to watch the family in front of them, frolicking in the turbulent sea. Andy wiped his mouth with a serviette.

'Do you remember teaching me to swim?'

'You were scared of the water.'

'Everybody's scared. At first.' Andy tried to sound authoritative, but his words were swallowed by the wind. He wondered if his father knew what power he had over him—how his entire self-worth could dissolve with as little as a word, a pause, an inflection in his father's voice.

'You were right to be scared. The sea is dangerous and unpredictable.'

As he spoke, Andy understood that when his father saw his cousins leaping and yelping in the water, he didn't see carefree summer holiday fun—he saw recklessness and stupidity.

'Everything is dangerous,' his father said. 'Wind. Water. Heat.'

Babies, Andy thought.

'Even birds,' his father added.

Just then a seagull landed on the patch of sand beside their towels. It eyed the chicken wings on Andy's plate. His father shooed it away.

'You can't live in fear of everything,' Andy said, his voice wavering. 'I learnt to swim eventually.'

'Because I taught you.' Andy's father frowned at the ocean. 'Accidents are never really accidents. Think of a plane crash— you can always trace it to something. A tired pilot. A screw somebody didn't tighten properly. A seagull in the engine.'

Andy didn't like where all this talk was heading. He was grateful to see Winnie and the children climbing back up the beach.

'Not everything is preventable,' Andy said as the twins announced their arrival with a splash of water and sand.

48

Lately, Meg descended into sleep, and dreams, quickly. Tonight she dreamt she was lying on a hospital gurney instead of a bed. Four round lights shone like perfect moons above her head. She was having surgery, but she was awake. When she looked down at her abdomen she saw that her skin had been peeled away like a banana's. There was blood everywhere. It was splashed across the blue sheets and the white walls and the masks of the surgeons, who were not surgeons at all but unnamed members of Andy's family. There was music— the same 'Over the Rainbow' that they had played at her mother's funeral. When the song finished there was a wail, but not from Meg. She felt an extreme hollowness—as if she had emptied her bladder and bowels simultaneously—before

Andy's family passed around what was presumably a baby, swaddled in a white waffle blanket. She could feel liquid oozing from the hole in her abdomen and from between her legs and from the corners of her eyes. The man she assumed was Andy's father held the bundle out to her, as if it was her turn in some sombre game of pass the parcel. Meg took the package hungrily, relishing the feel of warm limbs and soft flesh against her breasts. But when she removed the blanket, it wasn't a baby that she saw. It was a parrot. An African grey parrot with a bright crimson tail.

Meg woke with a start and saw that her sheets were soaked with blood. The trickle between her legs had been real. This was not remarkable in and of itself. She'd had countless dreams of searching for a toilet only to wake up with a bursting bladder. What really surprised her was that when she touched her cheek, she found it was wet with tears.

It was five am. She would never get back to sleep now. She got up, put on her dressing-gown and shuffled down the hallway to the kitchen to make herself a cup of tea. While she waited for the kettle to boil, she peeked under Atticus's blanket. Unlike her, he was resting peacefully.

She called the GP at eight-thirty, as soon as they opened. The receptionist said they'd had a cancellation and could fit her in at nine o'clock. Meg slipped on the same summer dress she had worn to go to the beach with Patrick. She took a straw hat from the hook in the hallway and walked out the front door.

By the time she reached the surgery she was breathless

and sweaty. The air conditioning was a relief. She filled a tiny paper cup with water and sat down near the children's play area. She'd forgotten to take Panadol before her walk and now her knees were throbbing. She rubbed them. There was silver tinsel framing the noticeboard and Bing Crosby crooning 'White Christmas' over the speakers. A baby with a snotty nose was chewing blocks of Lego on the mat at her feet. A woman about Meg's age with plastic tubes in her nose wheezed on the seat beside her.

Just then a man came out of room number four with a pile of papers and a poker face. There was no telling what had passed between him and the doctor. Meg remembered sitting in the room with her parents when the neurosurgeon had told them that Helen would never walk again. As the doctor spoke, she'd felt the gravity and finality of his words and wished that she'd plunged her fingers into her ears and screamed *lalalalala* to drown him out, like she used to do when Helen annoyed her. But it was too late. She'd heard her sister's fate, and once she'd heard it, it couldn't be taken back.

Minutes passed. The snotty baby was now munching on a teething rusk and the wheezy lady was flicking through a magazine. Soon the doctor would poke his weary face around the door and yell for Miss Margaret Hughes. Perhaps right now he was reading the ultrasound report, his heart sinking at the prospect of a cancer diagnosis before morning tea. Or perhaps he would call her in, completely unprepared, and read the report for the first time in front of her. She wondered what he would do when it was over. Would he lie and tell her everything was going to be okay? Would he put his hand on her arm and say she'd had a good innings? Either way, she would never know. Because when the doctor finally called her name, Meg had disappeared.

49

Winnie called the lawyer's office as they drove home. Everybody in the car could hear the receptionist's bored voice through the speakers. There was an appointment free the next day and Winnie said they'd take it. After she'd hung up they discussed logistics. She would accompany Andy's dad and act as his translator. Craig would come too, to lend his legal expertise. Nobody said so, but Andy assumed he would stay home and look after the kids. He watched his father's body relax once it had all been organised.

In Australia it was Winnie who behaved like the older sibling—arranging appointments, taking control. Andy remembered the two deep lines, like cracks, that had appeared on Winnie's forehead the last time she'd visited

Hong Kong. There were no signs of those lines in Australia.

When they got home the twins were asleep. Winnie carried Maddie and Andy carried Marcus to their matching beds. Andy's father excused himself and took a shower, presumably to wash away the sand that had, despite his best efforts, crept inside his clothes. Andy lay on the double bed with the peacock bedspread, ignoring the 'Jesus Loves You' poster above his head. He wondered what Mrs Hughes was doing. He imagined her in the kitchen, drinking tea as Atticus paraded across the table. But perhaps he underestimated her. For all he knew she could be lying naked under her cream-coloured sheets with Patrick.

Andy presumed his father would sue for financial compensation. He tried to estimate how much the Rose Street house was worth. In Hong Kong only multimillionaires lived in houses, but Mrs Hughes didn't seem wealthy. The bungalow was run-down, and she'd once told Andy she'd been waiting two years to have a knee replacement through the public health system. Perhaps Ming would know—his father owned multiple properties in Melbourne. But it wasn't just the financial stress Andy was worried about. There was something fragile about Mrs Hughes—he'd seen it in her eyes the first time he'd met her. And it wasn't because she was old. He knew that fragility was not an inevitable consequence of ageing—his own grandmother had been fierce right up until her death at eighty-five. But Mrs Hughes was a different woman from his poh poh. The stranger with the knife had already left her shaken—he didn't know how she'd cope now if she were burgled by a friend.

When his father returned from the shower, Andy closed his eyes, pretending to sleep. He listened to the pad of bare feet, the metallic click of clothes being hung in the wardrobe. Most of all he listened to his father's sighs and groans as he moved about the bedroom. When he heard him leave, closing the door behind him, Andy opened his eyes. The curtains were paisley orange and the room had an apricot glow. Listening to the muffled sounds outside the room—the clatter of plates, the TV, the low rumble of adult voices—he had the impression there was more than just a timber door between him and his family. He felt like an insect trapped in amber, imprisoned and alone.

When he fell asleep, he dreamt of Mrs Hughes' funeral. Somehow he'd been invited even though everyone at the church was furious with him. It was an open casket and, one by one, guests took turns to say their goodbyes. When Andy reached the front of the line he felt a stabbing pain between his shoulder blades. He fell forwards over the coffin and came face to face with the body. Except it wasn't Mrs Hughes' face that looked up at him from the casket—it was his mother's. She was dressed in a silk cheong sam—the red one Andy recognised from her wedding photos—and her hair was swept up in a bun. In spite of the pain in his back, he felt a rush of euphoria. He'd never seen his mother look so peaceful. It may have been the work of the mortician, but Andy thought he even saw a faint smile on her painted lips.

He woke up when his father slid into bed beside him. It was dark and the house was quiet.

'What time is it?' Andy asked.

'Eleven. We tried to wake you for dinner, but you were fast asleep.' Andy's father sat up and fluffed his pillow before laying his head on top of it. 'Are you hungry?'

'No.'

His father turned onto his side then, with his back to Andy.

Andy concentrated on his breathing. He counted to three in his head. 'I don't think you should see the lawyer tomorrow.'

His father didn't respond—was it possible he'd fallen asleep that quickly? Andy had never told his father what to do before. The only protest he'd ever made was in the form of a pout and tightly folded arms. His insolent words hovered now like big black balloons above the bed.

'Whether she knew it or not, that woman put your life in danger.'

Andy had expected anger, but his father's voice was calm. If there was ever a good time for a confession, Andy thought, it was now, lying in the dark, talking to the ceiling, blind to his father's reactions. But he couldn't bring himself to do it. He listened to his father's breath as it grew slow and heavy with sleep.

50

Meg was breathless when she got home from the clinic. She collapsed on the lounge in the front room and stared up at the ceiling. Atticus was perched on a branch of the small brass chandelier.

'Why did you come back?' she asked, but for once Atticus was speechless. He flew down and perched on her knee. 'You're not going to be rewarded for your loyalty, you know. You're only going to be abandoned.' She scratched the back of Atticus's neck and he regurgitated some seeds into her lap.

Atticus had often vomited on Helen, but Meg couldn't remember him ever doing it to her before. Patrick was right when he'd told Andy it was a bird's way of showing affection. Meg had read it in a handbook about African grey parrots.

She took a packet of tissues from her handbag and wiped the vomit off her skirt.

'Mary, Mary, quite contrary,' Atticus chirped.

Meg picked the parrot up, cradled him with both hands and walked to the front door. Outside, she launched him into the air. She'd seen people do the same with doves and pigeons, but Atticus's wings only fluttered briefly before he came to rest on the birdbath. He dipped his beak into the murky water and shook his wet head.

'Go on!' Meg said and waved her arms. 'Shoo!'

Just then a man carrying a newspaper under his arm walked past the house and looked at Meg with a puzzled expression. She sat down on the steps of the porch. When she was sure the man was out of earshot she mumbled, 'You may be smart, but you don't know what's good for you.'

As if in defiance, Atticus flew down from the stone bath and walked up the gravel path towards her. He bobbed his head up and down in a rhythmic dance, his pale yellow eyes gleaming.

51

At five am Andy got out of bed and walked to the kitchen. He switched on the kettle and sat down on the dog-haired couch. He didn't hear his aunt creep down the hallway in her slippers.

'Trouble sleeping?'

Andy nodded.

Winnie pulled two mugs down from the cupboard. 'Coffee?' she asked.

'Yes please.' Andy watched his aunt empty a tablespoon of ground coffee into a glass plunger. 'I was going to make an instant one,' he said, 'but this is much better.'

When the kettle had boiled, Winnie filled the plunger. Seconds later, the smell of roasted coffee beans filled Andy's nostrils.

'It needs a few minutes to brew,' Winnie said, turning to face Andy and leaning her back on the counter. She was barely recognisable without her hair done—she looked smaller, less intimidating. They stared at each other in the dark until Andy couldn't bear the silence anymore.

'Auntie, please, convince Dad not to go to the lawyer.'

Winnie frowned. 'Your dad is like me—as stubborn as an ox. We get it from our father. You remember how grumpy your yeh yeh was before he got dementia.' She turned back to the coffee and gave it a quick shake before slowly and carefully pushing down the plunger.

Outside, the sky was lightening. Andy could just make out the shadow of the cubbyhouse, the hanging rope ladder.

'Here,' Winnie said and handed him a coffee.

'Thanks,' Andy said, taking the mug with both hands. He moved to make space for his aunt on the couch and she sat down beside him.

'You need to tell him what happened. He's your father. He needs to know.'

Andy traced the mouth of the mug with his finger. 'I can't. He's not like you.' Andy thought of his uncle throwing the twins high in the air. 'I look at your family and wish things could have been different.'

Winnie laughed. 'You think I know what I'm doing? Most of the time I'm terrified. I have absolutely zero control over my emotions.' She stared at a point in the distance as if remembering something. 'One minute I'm playing with them like a good mummy, and the next minute I'm flying into a mad rage, screaming.'

Andy thought of his mother, and the feather duster she'd used to beat him. 'I think you're doing okay.'

'I've made plenty of mistakes.' Winnie put her hand on Andy's arm. 'Just like your parents. Bigger mistakes, probably.'

He searched his aunt's face. It wasn't like her to be self-deprecating.

'I should have driven to Melbourne to visit you.'

Andy remembered seeing Winnie that day at the café, laughing and drinking. He recalled how alone it had made him feel after everything that had happened with Kiko. But he didn't want his aunt to feel bad. 'I'm not your responsibility.'

'I don't mean it like that—you're not a burden. I just mean I should've been thinking about people other than myself.'

It struck Andy that his aunt spent most of her days thinking of people other than herself—cooking and cleaning for the family, looking after the twins, ferrying them to and from their various after-school activities.

'Anyway,' she said, patting his knee before standing up, 'you should tell him. It might even feel good to get it off your chest.'

Andy didn't go back to bed straight away. He watched the sun creep across the floorboards. He knew his aunt was right. Secrets were like cancer—they could devour people. He wished he were more like his father. His father would never swallow a bottle of sleeping tablets. He'd been through worse things than Andy—a sick wife, the death of his parents, the collapse of his cleaning business—and he'd weathered it all, like an old tree through a storm. But Andy wasn't like his dad. He was weak. Not weak with illness like his mother, or weak with old age like Mrs Hughes—just weak. A coward.

When the sunlight was lapping at his feet, Andy washed his cup in the sink and tiptoed back to bed. His father was still asleep, and somehow Andy managed to doze off. When he woke it was to children screaming, adults shouting and the violent slamming of doors. His father came into the room, looking frazzled.

'What's going on?' Andy said, sitting up.

Andy's father was dressed in a shirt and pants, but his hair was wet and he was carrying a towel. 'Your aunt and uncle are fighting. I don't think we can stay here much longer.'

'Really?' Andy wondered if this meant his dad would have to cancel today's meeting with the lawyer.

'We're putting pressure on your aunt's marriage by being here. After the appointment this morning, we'll go back to Melbourne. I'll follow things up from there.'

Andy felt something hard and cold, like a stone, form in his stomach. 'Dad, I have to tell you something, about the old lady.'

'Save it for the lawyer.'

Andy could hear his pulse in his ears—loud and fast and fierce. 'But you don't know the whole story.'

Out in the hallway, the twins were fighting over a toy. There was a shriek and a thump followed by an unsettling silence. Andy's father opened the bedroom door and peeked outside. Seeing nothing of concern, he closed the door.

'Your aunt doesn't know how to raise children,' he whispered when he turned back to Andy. 'She's not firm enough with them. She loves them too much.'

52

It was late afternoon. Meg was lying on a towel beneath the jacaranda. Above her, purple flowers lowered their tiny purple heads. She closed her eyes. Ever since the ultrasound, she'd been feeling overwhelmed. The other day she'd turned the radio on and a piece of classical music, one she hadn't even known the name of, had prompted a flood of tears. She spent most mornings on the couch in the front room with a book, watching Atticus hop from bookshelf to mantelpiece to windowsill, feeling the roughness of the book's pages beneath her fingertips and the softness of the cushions beneath her toes. It was exhilarating and exhausting.

Now she spread her arms wide and ran her fingers through the long grass. The earth was warm—she could feel its heat through her palms. She focused her attention on an ant meandering up the back of her hand. She listened to the coo of courting pigeons and the rumble of a faraway tram. She supposed she was practising the mindfulness Anne had always been going on about. Anne had travelled to workshops all over the world to learn how to master it.

Meg groaned as she sat up. Recently the pain in her pelvis had been growing more intense. As she bent her knees she heard a crack and remembered Andy's word for it—*crepitus*. She wondered how he was going in Geelong with his father and his aunt. She wondered if his family knew what had driven him to gulp down all those sleeping tablets. She wondered what dreadful thing the boy could possibly have been facing that had made death feel like the best option.

Looking back now, Meg wished she had talked to people more—not small talk but proper conversations. Discussions about life and death and God and the universe. Instead she'd spent her entire life doing what everyone else seemed to be doing—what she and Helen had, in turn, spent years teaching Atticus to do. Talking without really saying anything.

53

By the time Andy and his father appeared for breakfast, order had been restored. Craig was dressed and making a coffee in the kitchen. The twins, in uncharacteristically quiet fashion, were eating cornflakes with their heads bowed over their bowls. Andy couldn't see Winnie, but he could hear the whirr of her hair dryer in the bathroom.

'You're sure you're right to look after the kids for a couple of hours?' Craig asked Andy between sips of his coffee.

Andy nodded.

'Probably the best contraception a man can have is looking after these two little monsters!' Craig said and laughed.

Andy's father smiled politely. Andy knew he couldn't understand a word Craig was saying.

'Finished!' the twins said in unison before pushing back their chairs and running from the table. They ran so fast they almost knocked Winnie over as she walked through the doorway.

'Whoa!' she said with her hands up in mock surrender. 'What's the hurry?'

The twins cackled, and Andy wished he could run away with his cousins.

'We should get going soon if we want to make the appointment,' Winnie said as she picked up the empty cereal bowls. She wiped down the table with a sponge. 'We're still going to the appointment, aren't we?'

Andy sneaked a look at his father.

'Of course.'

Andy felt his aunt's eyes on him. His stomach was churning so much he worried someone would hear it.

'All my life,' Andy's father said in Cantonese, 'I've been getting pushed around—that's how I lost the cleaning business.'

Andy watched Craig slink away with his coffee.

'She's an old woman,' Winnie said. 'Something like this could destroy her.'

'She put my son in harm's way,' Andy's father said.

Winnie rinsed the sponge in the sink. 'It wasn't intentional.'

'People should pay for their mistakes.'

When Andy glanced up he saw that his father was glaring at Winnie. For once his aunt looked defeated. She turned off the tap and wiped her hands on a tea towel. Andy knew then that he was on his own. If anybody was going to stop this, it would have to be him. But the words were stuck in his throat. Unable to bear the stress anymore, he ran to the bedroom and slammed the door. Nobody followed him. He lay on the bed and stared at the wall. A few minutes later he heard a buzz on the bedside table. His father's phone. It was his mum.

He pressed the green button. 'Hello?'

There was no answer, but after a few seconds Andy could hear a quiet sobbing.

'Ma?'

More sobbing.

'Is everything okay?'

'I'm fine. How's your study?' She blew her nose into the receiver.

Andy could feel tears forming at the corners of his eyes. He pulled a tissue from a box beside the bed. 'Okay.'

'Only okay? Okay won't get you into medicine.'

'Study's good.'

'Your father insisted on seeing you. He said you needed help moving house.'

'I couldn't stay at the other place,' Andy said. 'Too many allergies.'

'I saw something on TV the other night about how Australia is the allergy capital of the world. They said when people from Hong Kong move there, they get bad allergies too.'

Andy wanted to ask his mother how she was sleeping, whether she'd be getting out of hospital soon. But it wasn't the done thing. 'How's the weather? Is it getting cold?'

'It's polluted. I can barely see my hand in front of my face.'

Andy looked through the window at the cloudless sky. 'I might come home, with Dad, for a holiday.'

'Flights are so expensive this time of year. What about study?'

'It's just a holiday. Dad says it's going to be okay.'

'Your father always says it's going to be okay. When you were born and we had nothing, he said everything was going to be okay. When your yeh yeh moved in with us, he said everything was going to be okay. When your yeh yeh died, he said everything was going to be okay. When the cleaning business collapsed, he said everything was going to be okay. Okay, okay, okay, okay, okay.'

Just then Andy's father walked into the room. Like a child caught red-handed, Andy held out the phone. They could hear his mother shouting the word *okay* over and over and louder and louder through the speaker. Andy's father took a deep breath and began the slow process of soothing his wife. Mostly he said nothing. Sometimes he made a grunting noise to show he was still listening. After he hung up, he sat on the side of the bed and buried his head in his hands.

Andy wanted desperately to reach out and touch his father—to soothe him in the same way he had soothed his mother. But he didn't know how.

'Your mother thinks I'm weak,' his father said.

'She's not well.'

'She's honest when she's not well.'

'You're not weak.' Andy stopped short of saying, *You're the strongest person I know.*

'That's why it's so important to stand up for yourself, to

stand up for your rights. I'm trying to teach you an important lesson. One I should have taught you a long time ago.'

Andy felt the panic wrapping itself around his chest.

'I know you feel sorry for the old lady,' his father said, 'but it's not right—'

'I need to tell you something.'

'Whether it was intentional or not, you've suffered. We've all suffered.'

'Dad.'

'She made a mistake.'

'I made the mistake!' The words exploded through Andy's lips. He'd never shouted at his father before and the shock of it stunned them both into silence. Andy looked at his dad. Rather than anger, Andy saw confusion on his father's face.

Andy told him about the overdose. The first few words were difficult to get out, but with each sentence it got easier. Partly because his father didn't move or react in any way—it was like talking to a wall. Andy told him how Mrs Hughes had discovered him. He told him about Kanbei and the two thousand dollars he'd been willing to pay to cheat on his exams. He even told him about Kiko and how she'd stood him up at the Vietnamese restaurant. The more he said, the lighter he felt. It was as if the words had weight, and they'd been holding him down all this time. His father didn't interrupt or ask questions. After a while Andy forgot he was talking to another person, let alone his father. He became intoxicated with the freedom he felt with each new declaration.

'That's some story,' his father said when Andy had finished. His face was blank, his voice neutral.

'Mrs Hughes put me in danger, but she also saved me.'

His father didn't agree or disagree. Andy felt his body tense up again. He had confessed to his father to save Mrs Hughes. As big a relief as it was to get his story out, he didn't want his sacrifice to be for nothing. He needed his father to see that none of this was her fault.

'I guess these things run in the family,' Andy said.

'You're talking about your mother.'

'I ruined her life when I was born.'

'That's not true.'

Andy clenched his fists, braced himself. 'You never had another child, because of me.'

There was a long pause. 'Your mother always wanted another baby.'

Andy didn't believe him. 'She said she hated being a mother.'

'She didn't mean it,' Andy's father said. 'It's difficult to be a parent.'

Andy wondered if Winnie had ever told the twins they'd ruined her life.

'It was me who didn't want another child. But not for the reasons you think. It was true your mother's doctors warned against it, but that wasn't why.'

Andy's head was spinning.

'I didn't need anything else,' his father said. 'I had my son.'

The shame dissolved then, leaving Andy empty. He leant back against the head of the bed, saying nothing, looking at his father's slumped shoulders, savouring his words, listening to his breathing.

'No family's perfect,' his father said. 'Every family is broken. Even your laughing Auntie Winnie is having an affair.'

54

Meg was studying the will kit she'd bought at the post office when Andy called. The phone caught her by surprise—nobody called her anymore—but she was thrilled to hear his voice. Their last interaction, muffled by face masks, had been like something out of a horror movie. There was a forensic feel about the way his family had taken cautious steps down the hallway—their eyes wide and vigilant, their arms fixed close to their sides. Now he said he wanted to meet her, just the two of them, away from Atticus, at Café Bonjour.

When Meg hung up the phone and turned her attention back to the papers spread out across the breakfast table, she had a sinking feeling. Now she remembered why she'd avoided such things in the past. The will reminded her of everything she didn't have—her lack of assets, her lack of savings, her lack of friends and family.

She had some cousins in Adelaide, but they'd lost touch years ago. There was an aunt in a nursing home somewhere in New South Wales, but the last time Meg had seen her was at her mother's funeral. Really, there was only Jillian. Meg reassured herself that this was still more than some people had. At least Jillian would make the house beautiful—painting it a special Scandinavian shade of white and filling it with proteas arranged in old jam jars—before selling it for an outrageous price. The good thing about Jillian was that she'd honour Meg's wish to sell it to a young family. More than anything, Meg wanted the old house to ring with noise and laughter again—to bear witness to another family's pain and joy.

What remained of her savings she would donate to a charity. The Paralympics, perhaps. Helen would have approved of that. As for Atticus—whom Jillian hated—Margaret planned on leaving him to Patrick. She was still haunted by the image of him in the waiting room that day at the hospital. She had a feeling Atticus would be good for him. She also knew that Patrick had a history of spending time with African grey parrots and she could be sure he didn't have a life-threatening allergy to them.

As Meg got dressed for her meeting with Andy, she had a sense of déjà vu. As badly as it had all turned out, she believed there had been something inevitable about her encounter with the young man. She was a different person now from the anxious woman who'd greeted him that day in a red blouse and sheepskin slippers. She was older, of course, but she was wiser too—they were not always the same thing.

In the kitchen she filled Atticus's bowl with seeds and gave him a quick scratch on the back of his neck.

'Better late than never!' he squawked.

Meg pulled down the blinds and closed all the curtains. It was forecast to be a blistering thirty-six degrees. She called a taxi. For once, it arrived within minutes. Thankfully the driver didn't begrudge her the short fare. She paid him, told him to keep the change—she could be reckless now—and stepped outside into the heat.

When she spied Andy through the window of the café, sipping a glass of water and jiggling his knee, she felt an unexpected wave of tenderness. She knew it was wrong to infantilise him—he was twenty-two and an adult—but she couldn't help it. She was next to the table by the time he saw her. He looked up and smiled.

Meg pulled out a chair. 'You look good. Healthy.'

Andy glanced down at his chest and hands as if noticing his appearance for the first time. 'So do you,' he said.

Meg knew he didn't mean it. She'd lost so much weight in the past month she'd had to take in her skirt with a safety pin. But she appreciated the comment. The waitress arrived then to take their order. Meg asked for a cappuccino and, after much prompting, Andy ordered a chocolate croissant.

'I'm so glad you called,' Meg said when the waitress had left.

'I wanted to say goodbye,' Andy said, taking another sip of his water. 'And thank you.'

'You're going home?' She shouldn't have been surprised, but she was. For some reason, she'd assumed Andy would continue with his studies, perhaps rent a room from another old lady.

'I'm deferring for a year. To recover. I'm going back to Hong Kong.'

Meg searched his face for fear or disappointment, but there was none. He seemed at peace with his decision. 'I'm happy for you,' she said.

'I'd like to send you something. Is there anything you'd like from Hong Kong?'

Meg thought for a moment. 'I'd like a photo of you and your dad eating those famous soup noodles.'

Andy poured Meg a glass of water. 'Is that all?'

'And a Chanel handbag.'

It took Andy a few seconds to realise Meg was joking. He laughed.

The waitress arrived with their order. When they were alone again, Meg drank her cappuccino and Andy picked at his croissant.

'Can I ask you something?' Meg said, after a few minutes had passed.

'Of course.'

'It may seem a bit silly.'

'That's okay.'

She cleared her throat. 'When you were unconscious all that time on the floor of the bathroom and in the ambulance, did you see anything, you know, strange?'

Andy's black eyes darted back and forth across her face, as if the answer lay in the web of her wrinkles. 'Is everything okay?'

'Everything's fine. Don't worry about it—I told you it was silly.'

Andy mopped up stray crumbs of pastry from the table with his finger. 'I don't remember anything. No visions. No bright lights. Nothing.' He flicked the crumbs onto his plate. 'It's as if the whole thing didn't happen. Like someone took a film, chopped out a scene, and stuck the two cut ends together.'

'Thank you,' Meg said. It was an intriguing, if unenlightening, explanation.

'Are you sure everything's okay?'

'I'm sure.' She waved to the waitress for the bill.

As they left the café, a large four-wheel drive pulled up in front of them. Meg recognised Andy's aunt by her big black bouffant hair.

'This is me,' Andy said. As he spoke, the passenger door opened and an elegant man wearing a neatly pressed shirt stepped out. Andy's father.

'Nice to see you again,' Meg said, and held out her hand. Her heart was jumping in her chest. She knew he blamed her for what had happened—she'd seen it in his eyes.

Andy said something in Cantonese. The elegant man stared at Meg's outstretched hand, and for a moment she thought he would refuse to take it. Perhaps he considered her to be contaminated too. But she was wrong. He took her hand in both of his and his gentleness surprised her.

'Thank you,' he said in English.

55

Andy slept for most of the nine-hour flight. When he woke up, the plane was making its descent. He felt his ears pop. The last flight he'd taken with his father was a couple of years ago, when he'd first moved to Australia for his foundation year.

His dad was asleep in the seat beside him. His head lolled to the side. Ordinarily Andy wouldn't dare stare at his father, but now he had the luxury of studying him—really examining his sleeping face. He looked older. There were new creases linking his nose to his lips and fawn-coloured spots on the crest of his cheeks.

Andy turned to face the window. Even though they were travelling at great speed, the plane seemed to be hovering—helicopter-like—above the clouds. He caught sight of his reflection. He looked different from the baby-faced boy who'd first arrived in Melbourne. He was more angular, more melancholic. More like his mother.

She would be waiting for them at the airport. That's what his father had said, but Andy had trouble believing it. He wondered how she would greet them. It was different every time. Sometimes she would grip his arm, tightly and urgently, as if she was being held against her will and needed his help. Other times she would launch into a bout of fussing, about his weight, and his clothing—worried he was too hungry or too cold. Mostly she would cry, sometimes hysterically but often silently, the fat tears spilling from her eyes unacknowledged and unexplained, by her or by anyone.

Just then, the plane hit some turbulence and Andy's father woke up in a fright. The seatbelt sign flashed on with a melodic ding. The flight attendants took their seats. Somebody started praying—a lone, steady beat amid the tremulous din. Andy was not religious. He'd told Mrs Hughes the truth at the café. But the truth was no comfort to him. He'd spent the past few years studying the human body—the astonishing way it worked, the thousands of horrific ways it could fail, the names of all the invisible organisms that could invade and destroy it. Andy had once confused such knowledge with power, with control, but now he knew it provided neither. It hadn't prevented him from taking those pills, or being attacked from the inside by his own body without his knowledge. Andy knew the passengers, including his father, felt that same kind of helplessness now. He also knew that when the turbulence was over, everyone would return to reading their books and watching their movies and playing their games as if nothing had happened.

Finally the captain's baritone voice crackled through the overhead speakers. He told them they were passing through an unexpected patch of bad weather. The pilot reassured them that the conditions in and around Hong Kong were calm. As they made their descent, ducking beneath the clouds, the aircraft stopped bucking and jolting. Through the window, ships dotted the sea like freckles. Every so often an island with tufts of green broke the rippled surface. Andy felt his father relax and spread his limbs in the seat beside him. Every so often the plane trembled and Andy felt their shoulders touch.

56

There was still half an hour until Jillian arrived to drive her to the clinic. Meg couldn't avoid the doctors any longer. Even if she'd wanted to, Jillian wouldn't let her. Not after that funny turn at the supermarket. Meg was lucky the security guard had given in when she'd begged him to call Jillian instead of an ambulance. Her friend's disapproving face was still preferable to the unrelenting questions she knew she would face from staff at the hospital. *Are you married? Who do you nominate as your next of kin? Who do you live with? Is there anyone who can pick you up?* Meg had worried she would see the pity mounting in their eyes and drown in it. At least the grumpy GP knew her history and wouldn't ask too many questions.

She was sitting in the backyard with Atticus. Ever since his escape, she'd let him roam free about the house and garden. If he wanted to leave now, Meg wasn't going to stop him. She watched him hopping on the grass, his crimson tail flaring in the sun. Above them a plane with a matching red tail soared high across the cloudless sky. Meg wished she had seen more of the world. It was too late now, which made her sad, but only in a vague, wistful way. It was not visceral and agonising, like the grief for her parents and Helen.

Meg surveyed the carpet of purple petals beneath the tree. Somewhere, buried within the soil, were her parents' and Helen's ashes. Most had probably been ingested by insects and transported away from the garden inside their little bodies, but some, certainly, remained there in the earth. When Meg died, hers would be sprinkled across the same spot, and not long afterwards the house would be sold to strangers. Nobody would visit her. Nobody would talk to her remains. When Jillian died, nobody would even know where her ashes were scattered. But just as she started to feel sorry for herself, Meg remembered the cemetery and the nameless graves with fractured headstones. Everybody was forgotten, eventually.

Atticus picked up a white stone from the grass with his beak. It glinted like a diamond. Meg leant back on the bench and closed her eyes. She let the morning sun warm her cheeks.

Soon she heard the blare of a horn. Meg picked up Atticus. In the kitchen she filled his bowl and returned him to his cage, leaving the cage door open. Jillian honked again. Meg grabbed her sunhat from the hook in the hallway. Before leaving, she looked back at the house— at its faded floorboards, warped at the edges; at its armchairs with cushions moulded to the shape of ghosts. Every face suspended in the dusty photo frames, except one, was now in the soil beneath the jacaranda. She reached behind her and found the light switch, her knotted fingers tracing the wallpaper like braille. There was a story here in the walls of this house— perhaps even poetry—but she didn't know how to read it. With a gentle flick of her thumb, Meg switched off the light.

ACKNOWLEDGEMENTS

Giving birth to a book shares some similarities with giving birth to a child. It's less messy, but—in my case, at least—it involves a comparable amount of stress, sleeplessness and muscle pain. I have been grumpy and impatient at times and first thanks must go to my children, Alyssa and Toby, who have consumed far too much takeaway and watched far too much TV this past year, and to my husband, Rani, for listening to me whinge, and for talking me through the frequent moments of self-doubt.

It was with great trepidation that I emailed the manuscript to my agent, Clare Forster from Curtis Brown, and my editor, Elizabeth Cowell from Text Publishing—partly because it is a terrifying thing to show your work to anybody for the first time, but mainly because I value the opinion of these two very smart and astute women so much. Thank you both for your belief in the novel and for getting back to me so promptly—it made for a much more relaxing holiday in Singapore! Thank you, too, to Michael Heyward for helping me realise my dream of publishing a novel and to all the team at Text Publishing for ensuring that the book reaches its readers. Packaging is of course important and I must thank W. H. Chong for enveloping my words in such a stunning piece of art.

I now understand that when you write a novel, you find your head bursting with obscure questions. Thank you to my mum for taking on the unofficial role of 'baby boomer consultant' (with help from her good friend Cath Nunan). Thanks to my dad for answering my left-field questions about Chinese language and proverbs (with occasional but essential help from my auntie Fanny). I am indebted again to Rani for reading the novel—his first!—in a couple of days and crosschecking the medical and hospital facts. Thanks, too, to the Sargents—Beth, Lynne and Graeme—for answering a last-minute query about education in Victoria.

I have been fascinated by talking birds ever since being introduced to my good friend Sive Bresnihan's African grey parrot during high school. The bird's name was Cindy, after her cinder-coloured feathers, and like Atticus, she was a character. I have only become more enamoured of these brilliant creatures since watching countless videos of them on YouTube. *African Grey Parrots: A Complete Pet Owner's Manual* by Maggie Wright was a particularly useful resource during the writing of this book.

Writing with children is hard. Thanks (again) to Mum and Dad for all the babysitting, and my in-laws—Haissam, Ahed and Dana Chahal—for cooking the kids' dinner every Tuesday and for devoting almost every Saturday night to me and Rani.

Lastly, thanks to my auntie Wendy, who was thrust into the role of carer at a young age and who remained a carer her entire life. She was one of those rare adults who could access imaginary worlds and play with the stamina of a fellow child. Dear auntie Wen, Meg Hughes was inspired by you.